## Advance Praise for *I Am The River*

"A sense of being hunted, and haunted, hits you right from the start of *I Am The River*. That mood only grows in intensity as the scope of this novel's nightmare takes shape. It's supernatural and geopolitical and an unforgettable time."
– **Victor LaValle, author of** *The Ballad of Black Tom*

"Grau's poetic prose and stunning evocation of time and place…from the killing fields of Vietnam to the haunted alleyways of Bangkok, form a fever dream of copious bloodshed and many shades of gray."
– *Publishers Weekly,* **starred review**

"*I Am The River* is the kind of thing that might happen if Algernon Blackwood had been brought in to do a rewrite of *Apocalypse Now*. A man barely holding onto his sanity in Bangkok remains haunted, stalked by a huge hound and undone by his own addiction. His only way out is through revisiting his past in the Vietnam War and the secret PSY-OPS mission he was involved in–and which he's been running from ever since. A haunting meditation on war, death, addiction, and responsibility, with mind-blowing forays into the weird."
— **Brian Evenson,**
**author of** *A Collapse of Horses* **and** *The Warren*

"With echoes of *Apocalypse Now* and Peter Straub's *Koko*, T.E. Grau's blazing, immersive novel takes us on the hell-ride of the Vietnam War's last days as its raging waters also carry us through the first of our last days. *I Am The River* is a hallucinatory tour de force."
— **Paul Tremblay, author of** *A Head Full of Ghosts*
**and** *The Cabin at the End of the World*

"An intelligent accumulation of inner and outer darkness."
– **Adam Nevill, author of** *The Ritual*

"A lush green nightmarish journey into the dark, reminiscent of the late, great Lucius Shepard."
— **Ben Loory, author of *Tales of Falling and Flying***

"*I Am The River* is a horror novel, yes, and it never skimps on its mission to unsettle us. It is also a book that finds horror not only in blood and shadows, but in the very real abysses that separate us: race, culture, and the manipulations of people by governments and by war. It moves quickly and intelligently from its first page to its last, evoking its nightmares in gorgeous, evocative, disturbing prose. A must-read!"
– **Christopher Coake, author of *You Came Back***

"*I Am The River* moves with fluid grace, flowing between times, places, and perspectives as it carries us through its protagonist's surreal experience of the Vietnam War and his part in a covert mission which refuses to loose its grip on him. Located at the hot, humid intersection of O'Brien's classic Going After Cacciato and Coppola's Apocalypse Now, this novel plunges us into war at its most extreme and insane, when the methods employed for defeating the enemy leave reason behind for terror and myth."
– **John Langan, author of *The Fisherman***

"Hallucinatory, gripping and haunting, *I Am The River* should rank as one of the best novels of 2018. The masterful point of view shifts and often stream-of-consciousness pacing makes for a riveting, oneiric read. In the author's hands, this bleak, nightmarish and deeply unsettling tale is not only palatable... but delectable. Of course, I expect such quality from Grau. Everything he has written heretofore is bizarre, literary gold. That stated, this book represents Grau's best work to date, and it is a must read."
— **Jon Padgett, author of *The Secret of Ventriloquism***

## Other Work by T.E. Grau

The Nameless Dark

They Don't Come Home Anymore

# I
# AM
# THE
# RIVER

## A Novel

# T.E. GRAU

LETHE PRESS
AMHERST, MA

Published by LETHE PRESS
lethepressbooks.com

ISBN:
978-1-59021-445-9 paperback

Cover created and designed by
IVES HOVANESSIAN

Interior design and cover layout by
INKSPIRAL DESIGN

This story is dedicated to Lewis Minor, Gene O'Neill, and to the surviving veterans of the war in Southeast Asia who fought and bled under their respective flags and motivations. This story is also dedicated to all those who were lost, those who lost something, and those who were left to wander. May each find their way home.

Special thanks to Paul Minor for the dossier and the plane ticket, and to Steve Berman for providing a secure home for my work. And eternal thanks to Fish for your conversations with the stars; and to Ivy, for the Martinique, and for absolutely everything else that matters in this world.

"A river of fire was flowing, coming out from before him. Thousands upon thousands attended him; ten thousand times ten thousand stood before him. The court was seated, and the books were opened."
—Book of Daniel: Chapter 7, Verse 10.


"War was always here. Before man was, war waited for him. The ultimate trade awaiting its ultimate practitioner."
—Cormac McCarthy, *Blood Meridian,*
*or the Evening Redness in the West*

# Chapter One

## Waiting Rooms

I need to hide in plain sight, here at the dead center of the world, for just a little while longer. I need to go unseen by everything looking for me, and it's a long, distinguished list. Things want me dead that you wouldn't believe.

So here I hide, sitting rail-straight in my chair, crooked spine upright, organs aligned and hands on knees, not moving a muscle as every fiber inside me wants to stand up and scream confessions. I tested the chair before I sat down, because I'm always careful, no matter how far gone, and found that it was a creaky chair. That was unfortunate, because I knew that when I sat down I'd have to remain still as a statue until my name was called. Don't give away the shake of the hands, the twitch forming in the left corner of my mouth, the side that always took the punch. Any quiver will be misconstrued as something other than what it really is. I need to be invisible, as they mustn't see inside me, and the heavy thing hiding in my right front pocket.

Three hours and forty-two minutes I've been sitting this way, the picture of patience and desperate camouflage, blending in with the cracks in the wall. The doctor would see me last, because I was an *estrangier* and demanded the extra scrutiny. A ripening underneath a secret gaze. In the careful game being played, anything outside the norm was made to wait, in hopes that if it was found perfidious, it would eventually disappear.

The air is bad in the waiting room and the lighting worse, with dim illumination provided by a crooked lamp in the corner and a filthy aquarium slowly suffocating a sweet corn goldfish so fat its dorsal fin never drops below the surface of the water. No table. No magazines. Not even a rumor of air conditioning during the hottest monsoon on record— one that inspired the old timers in the street to declare the end of this world and the beginning of another as soon as the earth cooled. Those who wait are made to suffer if they want relief. None of that candy-ass American dreaming for paying customers along Yaowarat Road, because what they're offering in certain shopfronts and office façades in Bangkok's Chinatown has enjoyed a seller's market since man dropped down from the trees.

I feel the eyes on me like I do everywhere I go no matter where I am, but I don't turn my head to see who's watching, or what. It could be the young woman with three well-behaved children sitting to my left, next to the ancient couple that have looked at each other for so long that they've remade themselves in each other's image. Or the man in the pressed trousers pretending to sleep two chairs to my right. He might be hired muscle, or a government proxy. Usually the same thing. But most of all, I don't want to see the other pair of eyes on me, that have been watching me from the inside the fog that morning at the edge of the jungle, when those two holes opened up for the first time and found me like a blind newborn worming toward its mother's breast. It's followed me ever since. Moving with me by day, coming to me at night. I know they're watching me now, daring me to turn and see and then lose my shit, just like the first, the second, and the third time I was stupid enough to act against my wiring and look deeply at what no man should ever see. I'd learned since then, because my grandmother didn't raise no fool no matter how hard I tried to prove her wrong, and on the fourth time, in that piss alley in Hue where I hid myself away from any new angles for so many days, hoping to die without making the move, I didn't look at the eyes when they found me. I ran instead, and didn't stop until I was two countries away.

But they found me again anyway. Somehow I knew they would.

Right now, if this *is* right now and not some other time, I focus on the yellowed poster taped crooked to the wall across from me. It's written in Cantonese, like all of the signs down here. No Thai allowed in this lowdown imperialist takeover from the inside out. The ghost of Mao is out to eat the world, one village, one neighborhood, and one sham doctor's office at a time. I hear the murmur of water rushing in between the walls. Faintly at first, but the sound grows. I know there aren't any pipes in those walls, but there is water. There's always that water. I narrow my gaze on one particular symbol on the poster, concentrating, trying to stay where I am, held fast by each curve and slash. My body throttles the movement in my muscles, outer shell motionless in this creaky chair, waiting for the walls to erupt, spilling out the water that'll suck me backward into the River, taking me downstream to that other time that I can't escape.

The door to the interior office opens and a high-pitched voice calls out a name in a language I don't recognize. Her intonation sounds fuzzy, a bad radio signal, and sets my mind humming like a hornet's nest, drawing strength from the water in the walls. It's going to happen again, I realize, at the worst possible time. I'm here for a very important reason, and can't afford to fall back into the River right now. But the buzz, the static spitting from blown-out speakers, always means the same thing. Water pools around my feet, seeping into my shoes. I close my fingers over my knees, as if I can hold myself here in this place. The chair creaks as my leg muscles clench. More eyes find me, a number higher than those sitting with me in the waiting room, and not entirely divided into pairs. Most can't see the water. None of them see my hands.

*Not yet*, I call out to the River. *I'm so close.*

The buzzing increases, and the water rises. At my ankles now, cold and biting my skin, sending a tongue up my leg. The River never listens, because it has no ears, but its mouth is always open.

A figure passes in front of me, its bulk made black by the River, and my anchoring gaze on the yellow poster is broken. I blink as the lights grow more intense and blank paper bright. Back-in-the-world bright.

The tether flaps
and whips
at my legs
behind
me.


I'm in a different waiting room, leaning forward on my knees, hair shorter but head weighed down by the fresh mass of what recently crawled inside it. The weight in my pocket is now gone. My feet are dry, and the sound of the River recedes far behind me. I've been through this before, and I've been here before, yet every time is a surprise, as I notice something new, and live through it just a fraction differently each time.

In this room, I keep my eyes down, away from the far wall and the posters I *can* read, because I don't like what they say. My gaze is fixed to the floor. I haven't seen tile like this since the hospital back in Baton Rouge, the first time I left the bayou and came to the city to watch my grandmother die with her mouth wide open, her tongue sticking out like a crushed bird. The tile there and the tile here is bluish gray and flecked with silver. It looks painted, but must have come raw from the ground like that, polished up and shipped to Southeast Louisiana and Southeast Asia to cover up the bloody dirt that lies beneath both places. Industrial tile. American tile. The fluorescent lights make the silver dance. Or maybe it's just my eyes.

But how could it be? They're just trapped sacs of fluid wired with the proper receptors and trailing nerves like a Portuguese man-o'-war.

No, it's my *vision* that's different now. Peripheral is sharper and almost front-facing without moving my head. I'm a flatfish, a flounder squatting on the ocean floor, looking up and out in every direction at once as two orbs migrate into one. Eyes develop this clarity in ancillary vision when everything on every side is gunning to kill you. They can't help but widen their perspective to take in more angles where death awaits. Survival of the barely fit demands a metamorphosis, and a deal is struck with nature without any consultation. Evolution doesn't ask for permission first.

There is only one chair here, made of form-fitted plastic and painted metal that doesn't make a sound regardless of how I move, and the waiting room is more of a hallway. It's empty and clean, with people and machines humming on either side of it, behind closed doors, muttering and humming in unison with the engines that drive the entire base. There's no water in these walls, because the River is gone.

Out of the corner of my new bottom-feeding eyes, I see it, crouching in the hallway corner at my five o'clock. It always waits in tight intersections of flat planes, as if angles provide it the proper geometry to spin a web to hold it fast for as long as it needs. Watching spider, if a spider is what it really is, which it isn't. Not truly, not to me. I don't dare glance at it. I've never done so, even when I'm in bed and it's squatting on my heart and lungs. It's changed now, this thing, adapted to its surroundings. Watching me, as it has the whole way back from the jungle, when I ran and fell and hid and killed to save whatever is inside me that makes me who I am. To keep this particular mass of atoms intact and shaped in this particular way that allows me to believe that I'm real. Mama's boy. Grandma's boy. Bayou boy.

I didn't think it would follow me here, in this time before it found me with a million tons of military machines set up to protect a native son sent to murder strangers in a foreign land. But it follows me everywhere and every time. It knows what I knew, that I was just another screw in the engine that was easy to replace when I wore out. I was unprotected, never protected in that peculiar way that would do any good, and it knew it. They'd know how to protect me down in the bayou in this new war I was fighting. At least I still like to think that, but I never went back there after that day in the hospital, looking at my grandmother's tongue. They took me away and my own tongue changed inside my mouth. A little bit every single day I was away from my home, reshaping my atoms based on a new latitude. After a while, seven years on, I shed my skin and was reborn just in time to be shipped out, shiny and new on the outside. All that Louisiana mud went with that final layer of skin, even though I wanted to keep as much of it as I could, but you don't get to decide what stays the same when the transformation begins.

Didn't matter anyway. I was holding on to lies and promises and half-remembered dreams. I was too southern for the north and then too northern for the south. Too backwater for one, too in the books for the other. I didn't fit in anywhere anymore, so I enlisted. Second worst mistake of my goddamn life. The first was leaving the bayou. Allowing myself to be *taken*, then recast on the wheel. Mud to clay to brittle boy cooling from the oven. Lies or no, it was the last time I felt safe and alive. I can live a lie if I know I'm living. Being dead with truth means you just lost, fair and square.

But this thing in the corner is neither and it's both. It's dead and alive, and it wants to take me to where it dwells, somewhere between the two or maybe somewhere outside all of that mess. It wants to take me there and have its way with me. I'd live a lie if it meant staying away from that place, that thing, living with me where I can see it fully with all of my eyes. If I die, it'll take me there, or find me there. It will be with me, mostly dead but also alive enough to feel every bit of it for as long as time has left. I've got to stay alive. Stay here or stay there but sure as shit stay. Harder still, I've got to stay *awake*, because the mind drifts close to death every time the body sleeps. I've become expert to this fact.

The door opens and the doctor stands in the doorway. I get up from the chair, and it makes no sound as I do. My hands don't shake here, now, back then, but everything inside me does.

The man is a woman and is wearing a uniform, similar to mine but different in all those subtle ways that matter. No white coat, although I'm not sure if I expected that or not. I've never seen a psychiatrist outside of the funny papers, and funny papers didn't matter for shit outside of the living room, away from the safety of threadbare rugs and bowls of melted ice cream saved for Saturday mornings because the local market sold it cheap to the early birds who got off the overnight shift. Everything I thought I knew about the outside turned out to be wrong the day I walked into the hospital and never saw my living room again.

The doctor is wearing glasses that reflect the light from the hallway, making it impossible to see her eyes behind the lenses. I wonder what those eyes have seen and how they've been altered since arriving in this dragon-scale land that beat back the bully by sheer force of chin, losing every fight but winning the war. Those round circles of glass could be hiding eyes just like mine, afraid to stay open but more afraid to close because of what happens when they do.

I walk past the woman without any eyes and enter the office. The door closes behind us and I wonder what's still left in that hallway, waiting.

## Chapter Two

## Up Country

The aquarium maneuvered slowly through an ocean, bumping along a sea floor of dark sand and green coral caverns deep enough to swallow a house. Shapes moved in the gray water, living things that remained unknown and unknowable to those forces that would catalog them, cage them, and open up their insides, studying something that needed no discovery by weak minds that couldn't understand them anyway. An aquarium inside an ocean, a stage play trundling along in the shadow of the real thing.

Broussard watched from inside the metal and glass enclosure, wondering how long the lashed tarpaulin would hold back a trillion tons of angry water, jealous of every bit of dry land stolen from it by the never-ending creation game of plate tectonics.

On either side, kelp forests danced and bowed as they passed, not out of respect, but in a long-forgotten comedy that left them giggling as the two bony creatures bounced on by, sucking in air through lungs that could be filled and popped like year-old balloons left out in a summer sun. And still the water came, roaring and greedy, furious in a way that only eons of frustration can properly grow.

Broussard closed his eyes, feeling the weight of water waiting above him, wondering what it would feel like to be pulverized into mash by something normally so soft and harmless when it lacked organized marching orders.

"You ever seen rain like this?"

The driver's voice was carried on a cloud of cigarette smoke, and ripped Broussard from the bottom of the ocean and placed him squarely inside a stinking U.S. Army-issue jeep on little more than a game trail in an unnamed hillside in Quang Tri Province. He turned back to the window, and now saw everything differently. Just mud, just jungle.

"Yeah, I have," Broussard said, because he had in Louisiana and eight other places down south, and because not saying anything would only lead to more questions.

"Well, I ain't. Not even here."

Broussard wondered why anyone felt the need to ruin an illusion to say something so stupid, so pointless. The back of the man's head looked like a giant thumb with the nail pulled out at the neck.

"Something weird in the air," the driver said.

*Yeah, bullets,* Broussard thought, but didn't say it aloud because he wasn't like this guy at all.

Up ahead, only partially visible through the wheezing windshield wipers and the torrent of rainwater that was once an ocean, three Muong women with woven baskets strapped high on their backs led an elephant out of the bush and crossed the road. The huge beast progressed across the muddy track with such delicate grace that it looked as if it moved in slow motion. Sitting on top of the elephant was a man in a low, crow-beaked turban, a World War II-era German MP submachine gun resting in the crook of his arm. He watched the idling American vehicle through the rain as the elephant passed and melted into the green wall of jungle. Neither jeep nor man wanted to know if the other were the enemy. That would save for another day. A drier one, perhaps.

"Goddamn gook tanks," the driver muttered. "We should shoot 'em on sight."

Broussard exhaled as he sat back and closed his eyes. Just minutes ago, before the cloud of smoke and the human thumb's meaningless words, before the crash and recede of the ocean into rain and jungle, Broussard would have seen a sperm whale escorted by three dark haired mermaids and a triumphant Poseidon, trident resting easily across his lap. Elephants were impressive, but whales and mermaids and water gods always took the prize.

"Lord fucking help us if we get stuck out here," the man said, lighting up another cigarette. "Don't let them maps fool ya. This is dink fucking central." His eyes squinted into the jungle on either side of the vehicle. "They're everywhere, even when they're not. Know what I mean, champ?"

The jeep continued up the rough track, packed hard as concrete by five thousand years of bare feet and unshod hooves. No one was getting stuck here unless the jungle commanded it. So far, it hadn't wanted their jeep, or these two fish inside of it. Like the people and the animals born of this land, the jungle wanted them to pass on through and leave everything alone. But like a jilted suitor, the United States military just couldn't do it. Couldn't leave well enough alone.

Back inside his body again, every bone ached from the six-hour trip out from Quang Tri Combat Base to meet up with his new posting at Con Thien Fire Base, which was the westernmost outpost of American influence in the province. Broussard still had no idea why he was being driven this far out away from his platoon that was getting resupplied at Camp Carroll. No one would tell him anything other than he was being transferred away from his company. Broussard had expected this, after what had happened at Hill 407. He also expected to be sent home for a reckoning after sitting in a cell for three days, ignored and barely fed. But he was released without ceremony and sent back into the bush on verbal orders. Nothing in writing. This had made him nervous, but seemed a better alternative than a military trial, so he shut his mouth and headed out into the jungle again, hoping for shit duty hauling sand or driving trucks and a quiet end to his unspectacular service in Vietnam.

Broussard wasn't cut out for any of this. Even after the shrieked indoctrination of boot camp, which he managed to weather without incident nor much distinction, he felt the violation of this country by his own. By *him*. Something didn't click about the American mission here, but he did what he was told. What other choice did he have? Swallowed by dead ends and ignoring the nightly news and the voices in the streets, he'd voluntarily placed his fate into the hands of the U.S. Army, and he'd do what he had to do to see this relationship through 'til the end. He wished he was stronger, but knew that he wasn't. He feared death. Feared killing even worse. They were the twin horrors. Monstrous and final, and totally unknown in their outcome. The M-16 by his side, the .45 in his holster, seemed like strangers to him, even though he was trained to see them as lovers, saviors. They just felt like cold metal, pieces of something forced and unnatural. He shouldn't be out here. He shouldn't be here at all. Hill 407 had made that all too clear. Sooner or later, he'd either get someone else or himself killed. Worse, he'd kill somebody, paying off all that training, with bloody interest. Broussard wasn't sure if he'd be able to handle that, and his uncertainty at his reaction terrified him. What would he do? What was he capable of doing?

The rain slackened, then completely shut off, leaving the inside of the jeep deafeningly quiet. The driver leaned forward against the wheel and looked up through the windshield. The world turned green again, the sky a mash of angry smoke.

"God must've pissed himself out," he said.

"God don't live out here," Broussard said, more to himself.

"You best hope he does, champ, or else we're *all* going to hell."

## Chapter Three

## Black Shuck

I brought a dog back from the jungle. A great big hound, five foot at the shoulder, shaggy black fur, built like a German shepherd but the size of a grizzly bear. Jaws always dripping wet, working those teeth, holding back the tongue. Yellow eyes sitting high on a skull the size of a bull heifer's. I've never seen the dog, not face to face, because I can't open my eyes when it comes near, but I know it looks like this because my mind tells me that it does, when my brain is the only thing free and my body is wrapped tight with chains. The antennae curled up inside my head sketch out the shape, and the details are filled in by the weight of its paws. It sits on my chest at night and does a downbeat match to the rhythm of my breathing, in for out and out for in. The dog breathes corruption into my face, pushing out all the rot it has inside it, everything it's eaten, and then sucks away all of the good, clean air in the room, leaving me with nothing when it's my turn to breathe. It's heavy, this beast, and my lungs can't expand much at all, so they do double-time, triple, in tiny heaves and grabs, looking for just a little bit of air to keep me from drowning in the River that has taken my bed, underneath the weight of that dog sitting on my chest, pushing me down into the water. That burning River, surface littered with flame.

Black Shuck is its name. It didn't tell me this, because I can't get enough air to make a sound when it's sitting on my chest. Someone else told me this name a long time ago, a swamp witch named Arceneaux with wide-set eyes and hair that looked like fireworks frozen in mud. I didn't believe that Black Shuck was real, because everyone knew that the swamp witch told lies to scare all the good Christians and get coins from the devil for each bit of badness she let loose into the world. But I believe her now. Black Shuck is real and he comes to see me at night and he's sitting on my chest right now.

I brought a dog back from the jungle, and that dog wasn't Death but something older, meaner. And right this very second, this old mean thing is trying to kill me.

The panic of drowning detaches what's left of my soul and I float above the situation, letting me size it up just one more time for posterity, because I know this is it. It has to be, because I can't take any more.

There I am down below, and there it is, all of its forms in one. I still can't see its face but I don't need to. The bulk of the thing is enough.

It isn't always a dog on the outside, I've noticed over time, but a dog is what it is. It was a woman once, my mind tells me. Probably Arceneaux but probably not, because the weight of it didn't feel like that old weird swamp woman. It felt heavy, like every girl I ever wanted but couldn't have, all sitting with the combined burden of desire unfulfilled and fear never fully dealt with. Face full of taunts, eyes lit by hate, clawing at my closed lids. Those yellow eyes staring down at me. But I knew this was just Black Shuck, hound born in the void, weaned on black cream and taught knowledge from the echoed psalms sung to dead stars. It's not always a dog on the outside, but has a dog's habit of following after a man until one of them dies.

On the street, in the alleyways, in corner stores and a doctor's waiting room, Black Shuck takes a shape to help it blend in, to not attract any attention while I remain at the forefront of its every observation. Or maybe I'm just one of many it hunts. I have no way of knowing, other than what my antennae tell me. It might be thousand things, chasing a thousand souls.

But at night, with me, it's the dog, a half-ton hound perched on top of me when my eyes are closed, sagging the bedsprings and stealing my breath, waiting for me to expire so it can consume me with that huge wet mouth and take me back to its warren to feed its litter, or cast me out into the Great Nothing like scat squeezed into a lake.

I'm not sure how I feel about being eaten. Because I know it will happen eventually, I can't decide if I just want it to be over with, or if I want to experience each and every agony of being chewed and ground and rent asunder, because I know that it will be the last thing I really feel before the eternity of pure nothing. I don't know if pain is better or worse than wide-awake paralysis that persists until the end of everything.

I don't know because I'm a coward.

Big tough coward. Biggest pussy in the world. The war taught me that. No, not taught—*verified*.

Black Shuck knows this, what I didn't do back in the jungles of Vietnam, and what I did do in that jungle in Laos. How I did finally rise up when I needed to, and then rose up too far when I shouldn't have, when I could have just run with my bravery but instead killed with my cowardice. Its roiling consciousness tells me that it knows; its breath, carrying the stink of those bodies, and that one in particular. I can smell it. The coppery smell of muscle without skin gone bad for years.

This thing wants to kill me. Wants *me* to kill me. Either way, it wants me dead and then have me all to itself.

It's getting close tonight, because I can't breathe. I'm drowning in my bed, in the River that's risen up over my mattress while my body is wrapped in concertina wire. The smallest move will slice my flesh but I can't move.

Here it comes. The black is coming to take me, and I'm too worn out to fight it anymore. Too tired to use the fear anymore. The River is rushing upward, louder and louder as I sink down deep. It's wet and cold.

Through the sound of the water, I hear a knock on a faraway door. It's soft, the knocking, but it's enough.

Black Shuck is gone.

A knock on a door saves me. It scares away Black Shuck in all its manifestations, which reform and retreat back into it as it slinks off into the shadows where the wall meets the ceiling, a raspy voice and a growl combining with many whispers trailing behind it as it goes.

Maybe it's a coward just like me, scared of the outside world, those who aren't supposed to see it.

Big tough coward. Biggest pussy in the void. One more thing we have in common.

Another knocking, louder now. The door has come closer. It might be my own door, but it's difficult to tell, with the sound of the water receding under my bed, the bladed wire falling off my body and retracting into the floor. I'm still not ready to move, but I know that I can if I need to. My body hurts, my brain is on fire.

A third knock. I need to get up, and go pay tribute. Whoever or whatever it is saved my life. This time, anyway. The next time the hound comes and the River rises will be my last. It has to be. Neither of us can take any more.

## Chapter Four

## Birddog

"Wake up, Broussard."

Broussard raised his chin off his chest and opened his eyes, staring up at the canvas roof of the hooch, where a pink grass moth slowly flexed its wings. It was a patient movement, deliberate, and they thrummed with the sound of a colossus, chopping the air above it outside. Many wings, descending. It was terrible. Broussard felt the fluids inside of him vibrate. He closed his eyes again, waiting for it.

"Well I'll be goddamned," the voice said, thick Dixie accent bending the words just so. "I do believe you could sleep through the apocalypse."

Broussard sat up.

Tim Darby grinned, shirtless and sweaty like he always was, cheap jailhouse tattoos cut by jungle rot scars quivering like broken earthworms dying on wet cement. He was cleaning his rifle again, the third time today, each piece set out in precise rows. He was a tidy sort, this filthy man. Hard to get a handle on, all busy hands keeping away from the devil's business but probably planning something far worse inside his mind. Darby raised his eyebrows at Broussard, pointed two greasy fingers into the air, his smile growing as the sound increased, stirring up whatever was inside of him. It was a terrible thing to witness. "The angels of death have arrived!"

Broussard looked up at the tent roof. The moth was gone.

Willie Render entered the tent, walked right past Darby and grabbed his pack. "Come on, Crayfish, we gotta go."

Render called Broussard "Crayfish" because Broussard was from Louisiana, and apparently everyone from Philadelphia, where Render grew up, was entirely certain that people from Louisiana, and especially the bayou, ate crawfish for breakfast, lunch, and dinner, excepting Thanksgiving and maybe Christmas. Broussard didn't have the heart to tell him that it was "crawfish," not "crayfish," because he knew from firsthand experience that things were different up north, and the truth wasn't always clear about how things happened down south.

John McNulty, a pie-faced, packing-plant white guy from Chicago built like a loaf of Wonder Bread, had giggled about the nickname, muttering something about being a "bottom feeder…hiding under rocks." Render had threatened to kick his dumb cracker ass, so McNulty kept his giggles to himself. Being six-two and built like a middle linebacker—a position which he did in fact play at St. Joseph's Prep and two years at Temple before being drafted by Uncle Sam after blowing out a knee and a suspicious registration error at the school—got people into line double-quick, even dumb, pie-faced crackers like McNulty. Established lines broke down during war, and the laws of the jungle came back into play when all the blood leaking into the jungle was just as red and just as scared. Pure Darwinism, from the officer class on down. Probably from higher up than that.

Broussard looked through the tent opening, out into the swirling dust and noise sweeping the clay skull top that that made up Con Thien. "What are they?" he said, thinking of giant pink moths, hovering above the tents and ammo dumps, sucking up the insides of each structure with a long proboscis.

Render clamped his hand on the top of his helmet, fighting against the rising wind that blew through the hooch. "What?"

Broussard pointed outside, to the noise and swirl. "What's coming?"

Render laughed, the sound of it drowned out. "Our ride," he shouted as he stepped out of the tent.

"To where?" Broussard said. No one had told them their mission, nor who was their CO. The men had been muttering about it the last two days, in between talking shit and reminiscing about home, but all anyone—to a man—was told was to wait for their ride, and get on when it arrived. Broussard had assumed it would a truck, ferrying them to some shit job in the rear created to keep the castoffs occupied until the war was over. Why else was he let out of his cell back in Quang Tri?

"Does it really matter?" Darby said, fully dressed and geared up. How did he do that so fast? He clapped Broussard on the shoulder and peeled back a diseased grin of graying teeth crowded between tight lips. "You got somewhere else to be?"

Darby and Broussard jogged out of their tent, lugging their packs and rifles. Render, McNulty, and Jorge Medrano, proud son of the San Joaquin Valley, were waiting by the edge of the LZ, enveloped in purple smoke gouting from a signal grenade, whipped crazily by the gusts. They all held down their helmets and looked up, as three helicopters dropped from the sky at twice normal speed. A pair of Hueys flanked a CH-47 Chinook like sparrows fussing after a gliding hawk. All of them were painted black, and had no markings or numbers on the outer hulls.

The Chinook and one of the Hueys leveled off twenty feet above the ground. The remaining Huey dipped to the LZ, blades still spinning, landing skids barely touching the ground. The side door opened, and Render led the four others to the empty fuselage. Broussard couldn't take his eyes off the Chinook waiting above them, its heavy bulk motionless and imposing. It was an impressive machine, long and rounded, like a killer whale on land, insides hollowed out to fill with every sort of promise of death. Its doors remained closed, windows blacked out. Broussard wondered what lay sleeping inside its stomach.

Broussard climbed in after Medrano, and before he could find a seat and strap in, the chopper was gaining altitude. He fastened his safety belt and looked down at the fire base below him. A dozen GIs moved like lazy beetles over the top of the raw hilltop sticking out from the surrounding jungle like a Franciscan skull, denuded of bamboo by machete and Ka-Bar. Broad backs filled sandbags, dug 40x40 foxholes that would someday probably save their lives, burned trash in fifty-five-gallon fuel barrels cut in half, smoked cigarettes and adjusted the M110 eight-inch howitzers choppered in months ago to provide fire support for terrified grunts humping through the jungles below in a ten-mile radius. None of them looked up to watch this strange array of unmarked helicopters and their confused passengers leave them behind, almost as if they were never there. Ghosts passing through.

But the group of South Vietnamese ARVN troops who were hunkered down by the perimeter, squatting in their own holes and listening to a transistor radio, all looked up as the helicopters rose into the sky. Before the side door slid shut again, each one of them raised their left hand and made a gesture with their fingers. Broussard couldn't make out what it was at first, thinking it was a middle finger picked up through contact with the Americans. As the door sealed shut, Broussard realized they were crossing their fingers, which meant something far different in the land of the Blue Dragon.

## Chapter Five

## Night Man

The outside knocks at the door. The door is thin, but holds, at least for now. The knocks have saved my life. The door only saves my dignity.

I can breathe again. My lungs unfold and my arms and my legs come back to me while my brain waits and my heart remembers its rhythm. And still the knocks come at the door. Steady, not any harder or softer. Now that my life is saved, now that Black Shuck has been chased off by an intrusion from the outside world over which it has no domain, my fear shifts to those knocks. It could be anyone, but worse yet, it could be someone who can drag me from my cave and throw me into a hole, without my medicine, with only violence and sleep as my eternal sentence. Violence and sleep. The violence of sleep until the day I stand on the brink of the abyss and am carried away into the forever dark with it dragging me there by my ankles.

A hand knocks again. A small hand, by the force of it. I would leave these knocks alone, but I know they won't go away, and the racket will draw attention from those other kinds of eyes that are more than willing to snatch me up and put me in a cage. I'll be goddamned if I ever let that happen.

I let my feet find the floor, knowing that it's probably still covered in water of an endless depth that will swallow me like it tried to swallow my bed, weighed down by the hound. I step anyway, because I have to get off this raft, and toes come into contact with the dust and the damp. I stand, the wounds on my chest felt but invisible to daylight eyes. Mosquitoes circle silently in the air, just like in the jungle. They're not as big here, and they refuse to bite me, holding back their malaria and meningitis. Maybe it's the medicine in my brain, or the dreams in my head. Either way, they leave me alone, waiting for me to invite somebody else into the room so they can have their way.

The knuckles continue to rap at my door. This isn't going away. None of it, not even the mosquitoes.

I walk jungle-quiet to the door and listen. No voices, just the knocks. I peel back the locks, turn the handle and open the door. A withered old woman stands just outside, her granddaughter next to her, holding her hand and holding her up, as the old woman is near collapse from age or grief or some combination of both that keeps old people going long after they should.

The granddaughter looks vaguely Caucasian, hazel eyes imploring me to let them in and give them peace. Another abandoned legacy from the war, this girl, left like a valley crater or rusting M48 tank. The girl and her grandmother are Vietnamese, cut deep by war—refugees just like me.

"Night Man, hep us, okay?"

She speaks pidgin English that an outsider would think was probably gifted to her by her G.I. father. But I know that wasn't the case. She never met her daddy. Never knew his name or his face. He left or died before she was born, early in the back-story days of the war. Probably a contractor or CIA trainer, leaving behind one more colonial flag buried in the clay. Her English comes from pirate American radio and British Invasion records.

I look down at the girl, barely in her teens. She's skinny but certainly thicker than any other girl in her family or on her block, with what was probably Scandinavian stock that filled out her hips and lightened her hair to a shiny bronze instead of a silken black. She's an outcast just as much as I am, which makes her suited to life down in the Floating City. *No child, your daddy never saw you born, never held you up like the gift you are.*

"You hep us, okay? We pay."

She holds up a covered bamboo basket. They never bring any cash. They bring trade. Food, family heirlooms, a chicken raised in their kitchen. The purest Triad heroin in the world, that would go for a cool grand in New Orleans or Harlem, but is cheaper than cooking oil in this neighborhood. Even with my employee discount, I can always use a little more junk, one half of an equation that has kept me on the edge of the abyss for going on four years. But she brought a basket, probably filled with something rolled and baked and totally worthless to me. I need cash, and I need sweet and sour white powders, and I need answers, and none of these things are standing in my doorway today.

The girl points to her grandmother. "See her dreams, Night Man. You tell."

*Người đêm*, they used to call me, before. When I first stumbled down the street below and climbed up into my cave. *Người đêm*. I could barely get my tongue around it, even in my head. The older Thai, and the Vietnamese who never went back home even after all of us left, would mutter more quietly in French, putting a name to the man who had lost his. "*Homme de nuit.*"

Night Man.

A legend had wrapped itself around me, just another dark fairy tale of the Floating City. People told me about it, the ones who could speak English or whatever passed for it. I never asked, but they'd tell me anyway. They said that my body turned brown like a rotten fruit when I died, digesting itself, and that I didn't know I was dead. Others said that I was once a brilliant white—my hair, my skin, my eyes, my heart—but I'd spent too much time on the Other Side, was dipped too long into the abyss, and now I was black inside and out.

Night Man, they call me. The transformed freak who can see their dreams, read their future, find the lost souls.

"You go…" The girl pushes on the old woman, who doesn't move. "*Insi.*"

The old woman, who doesn't know any English, who won't lower herself to speak what French she does know, gets her toothless mouth around the word in her ancestor's tongue. "*Người đêm.*"

I close the door on them both.

## Chapter Six

### The Weight of Paper

I sit in the soft chair, sinking half a foot. The doctor is positioned behind her desk, hands folded under her chin, and looks down at me waiting below her like a scolded child.

"I'm Dr. Massaquoi," she says, making it a point to mention her name so that I pick up on the Creole vibration that maybe wasn't expressed in the caramel color of her skin, the freckles that ease back from her cheek into the particular curl of her dark brown hair. Cutting that skin are the lenses of her glasses that reflect the light from the desk lamp, hiding her eyes. I need to see her eyes so I know what I'm dealing with, but that glass won't let me. An air-conditioning unit hums in the corner, cooling the room to the temperature of a morgue. Framed photos cover the walls, showing another doctor also wearing glasses standing next to other men in full military uniform. All of their faces look the same. I can't find the face of Dr. Massaquoi anywhere.

At the front edge of the mostly deserted desk is an egg-shaped paperweight, veined with a stringy blob of pink matter encased by heavy, bubbled glass.

"What do you see?" the doctor asks.

"A jellyfish," I answer.

Dr. Massaquoi waits for me to continue, but I don't, because there isn't anything else to say. She waits for a few seconds more, then a full minute. This is the game. I want the whole thing to be over with, so I pick up the paperweight and look at it closely.

"A jellyfish trapped in a bubble of air. Suffocating because it can't breathe like we do."

I look up at her and it's not her—now a different doctor from a different time. It's the man in the photos who looked just like everybody else.

"Just what happened out there, Specialist?"

I remember where I am, where the River has dropped me this time. This is my debrief after Signal Hill, when my eval report took a mortal wound from which it never recovered.

The doctor chuckles, leans forward and holds out his hand, palm up. It's not shaking. Why would it? The man hasn't seen or done anything his entire life aside from sitting behind desks and staring at people, making them feel small in tiny soft chairs. I put the heavy glass into his hand, dropping it a few inches. Can't take the weight. He carefully replaces the paperweight on the edge of the desk, settles back into his chair and regards me again, but I know he can't see me. No eyes behind those glasses.

"What happened out there, Specialist Broussard?" The voices of the two doctors have combined into one, musical and deep.

I look up, and it's Dr. Massaquoi.

"Why are you here, Specialist Broussard?" she asks.

"You don't know?" I ask in return. I know that she knows. I also know that this is just another part of the game, regardless of who's asking the question.

"Yes, I do know, but I'm asking you. That's how this works. You do want this to work, don't you?"

"They sent me here, just like they sent you."

"Who's they?"

I don't answer.

"Why did they send you here?"

"I don't know."

"Do you believe your superiors have a vested interest in your health, your well-being?"

"I don't know."

The doctor stares at me. The silence lasts so long that I feel like I'm going to scream if I don't say something, so I do. "I'm not sleeping."

"Insomnia. They flew you here, at great expense to taxpayers, because you're not getting your beauty rest?"

"I guess."

"And what is keeping you from sleeping?"

"I don't like it."

"The question stands."

"I don't feel like it's safe to sleep." I won't tell her anything more, because if I dig down into the truth, the God's honest, they'll lock me up and pump electricity into my brain.

"That's a conveniently vague response, don't you think?"

I shrug.

The eyebrows above the glasses are now bushy and belong to the other doctor, the man, who never told me his name because it didn't matter to either of us. These brows crowd low over his glasses. If he had eyes, they'd be squinting at me. "You wouldn't be trying to malinger, would you?"

"Excuse me?"

"You purposely didn't engage the enemy when given an explicit order," he says.

"I didn't see an enemy to engage with at the time."

"I see. So you're in command, I take it?" Both of the doctors sound alike. Not their voices, or their accents, which sound totally different. But what's underneath both reads like the same script.

"No, sir."

The chair creaks under the thin frame of Dr. Massaquoi as she sits back, looking up at the ceiling, where no mosquitoes collect in silent conference, as if this place is a thousand miles from the jungle. It just might be. The River moves quickly, and nothing can stop the current. "It's impossible to test," she begins, as if launching into an internal monologue translated with her mouth, "or even to adequately and quickly treat, what happens inside a person's mind, which is what I assume you're implying. That there's a problem inside your mind. What most military medicine classifies as 'psychosomatic.' Do you follow what I'm saying?"

*Oh, yes. Me speakie English real well.* "I'm just saying that I can't sleep."

"Yes, that's what you're saying," the other doctor says, turning in his chair. "But let's be honest, soldier, that's not what you mean when you say that, is it?"

"You're trying to twist my words."

"No, I'm not. I'm trying to get at the true *meaning* of your words, because you seem unable to provide that for me.

I try to stand, but the chair won't let me up. It's so low I can't find my feet. The carpet feels stick, wet with river water. I miss the tile of those hallways. "This was a mistake. I shouldn't have come here."

"No, it's not a mistake, and you had no choice but to come here. This isn't the army of Specialist Broussard. This is the Army of the United States of America. You serve. They command. They snap. You dance. That was the deal, and you knew the deal before they shipped your ass eastward."

I grit my teeth so hard I know he can hear my enamel pop. If he does, he doesn't let on. He steeples his fingers in front of his face like all the scientists do in the movies.

"So here you are, sent to me in hopes of proving something that isn't provable, not in any quantifiable way, in order to shirk your responsibilities, and abandon the soldiers in your squad. That presents quite the conundrum for the U.S. Army, doesn't it?"

"The soldiers in my squad are all dead."

Dr. Massaquoi leans forward in her chair. I can smell her perfume now, the scent of someone else. She'd never buy it herself. They added it later as a prop. "That we can't figure out who or what your squad was or is presents quite the conundrum for the U.S. Army, as well."

"That to me sounds like a U.S. Army problem."

"But your squad wasn't U.S. Army. Not even by the most loosely applied interpretation. This is a *you* problem, and will remain so until you give us some answers."

I look at the jellyfish again. Mush frozen in mush that hardened when it cooled. Ancient baby stuck inside a coffin egg, and we're all gawking at it.

"Just because the jellyfish is soft," a voice says, "it is a mistake to assume that it is harmless." The voice isn't from Massaquoi or the other doctor or their voices combined. I don't know whose voice it is.

"What did you say?" I ask, looking up at the doctor. It's the man doctor. Dr. Man.

Dr. Man frowns, puzzled. "I didn't say anything. You just did."

"No, I did, but then, someone else..." I stop and wait for the other voice to continue, but it doesn't. Was it me? The other me, outside the River?

"Is this part of the pantomime?" Dr. Massaquoi says. "The play at insanity to shirk your responsibility to your nation and to the truth of this rather serious matter?"

I continue looking at her, not really grasping her words, my mind still replaying what the other voice said.

She waves her hands dismissively, resetting the conversation. "Okay, I'll be direct, so you don't get confused, so you can't claim confusion, and so you *do* know what I'm talking about." She pokes her fingers down at the thin closed folder on his desk. "Why were you found in southwestern Laos, a country in which the United States military is not allowed to operate? Who took you there, and what were you doing, while violating international sovereignty and putting your country in a potentially embarrassing and dangerous situation?"

I scan the walls again with a different focus in these new eyes. No advanced degree or certification in sight. No medical license. Nothing medical at all. Just those interchangeable photographs. Just like I thought.

Faced with my distracted silence, the doctor presses on, like he did so many months ago. I know what he's going to say, of course, because he's already said this to me before I was sent to Dr. Massaquoi. "You're facing charges of cowardice in the presence of the enemy. Do you know what that'll do to your fitness report? Do you know that this means no fire team will take you, that your only option is a court martial and public humiliation?"

"You're not a doctor," I say to him. His eyes narrow, then open up again inside the skull of Dr. Massaquoi.

"Where were you serving, and with whom?" she asks. "Who was your commanding officer? What was your mission? Why does your file report you 'reassigned without comment' as of five weeks ago, with no record of a new platoon or any assignment at all? What was this reassignment?"

"You're not a doctor at all, are you?" I say to her, because she needs to hear it, too, even though she already did when she was Dr. Man.

Another smile, from both of them, in different pictures on the walls that I can't see. Each one of them tighter than the photographed occasion demanded, because they were smiling back from the future, and from the future forward, after both emerging from the River.

"You're the gutter dog, dressed like a lamb." I tell this to both of them, but only Dr. Massaquoi has the courage to hear it.

Her eyes flash behind those small circles of glass, colorless and cold. "Insults and metaphor all in the same sentence. I see I'm dealing with a very special sort, here." She picks up an orange that was resting behind the base of her lamp and regards it like Hamlet with old Yorick's skull.

When she speaks again, the doctor's—the officer's—tone returns to that practiced note developed in preparation for his role. "Why did Company Command send you here, Specialist Broussard? Why did they *really* send you here?" Here it is, the fourth quarter of the game.

"I told you, I don't know." If she's going to continue the charade, I can too. Free air conditioning is free air conditioning.

"No one is sent here without a very good reason, which most certainly does not include insomnia," Dr. Massaquoi says, opening up the folder, which contains only a few pieces of paper and some photographs. I have a good idea what those photographs are, but can't figure out how anyone got them. Nobody out there from our side was left, and without a witness, that ridge top would disappear back into the jungle without a sound. I'm the only one left who would know, and I don't. "Your file says that you are indeed here for a very, very good reason."

"If you say so."

"No, I don't say so, but your superior officers do. The field report does."

"They don't understand."

"They don't understand what?"

"They don't understand what...what happened to me. What's *happening* to me."

"Because you won't tell anyone what happened to you." She almost purred, sounding genuinely concerned. The River told me otherwise.

"Wouldn't help. I'm talking about now. After."

"And I'm only interested in then. Before."

"Then there's no reason for me to be here."

Dr.—Officer—Massaquoi exhales, smoothing out his impatience. "What *did* happen to you, Specialist Broussard? Out there. That might be the best place to start."

"We got overrun."

"Who's 'we'?" Dr.—Officer—Man asks.

"Our squad."

"Was it a squad?" Officer Massaquoi asks. "Not a platoon?"

I shake my head. She writes something down.

"This squad wasn't U.S. Army," she says, a statement, not a question. She's trying to lead from the rear, just like all the rest. She's clearly different from them, in their eyes and probably in her own, but she's just like the rest underneath.

I shake my head again.

"What branch? Under whose auspices?" Her pen is poised over the page. Seconds eat deeper into the fourth quarter.

I look straight ahead. I'm not even sure myself. Not totally. But I'm not telling her that. Motherfuck this traitor. Some things are thicker than duty, and one of them is blood.

"Why did you let your squad down?" Officer Man asks.

"I don't have an answer," I say.

"Who recruited you?" Officer Massaquoi asks. "Who organized this squad? Who was your commanding officer?"

*Augustus Cornwallis Chapel.* My mind screams these three names that make up one so loud I assume the woman they found to be the perfect ringer behind the desk can somehow pick them up with her own antenna. But my lips know to keep shut, *taisez-vous*, fight through that urge to empty my entire limbic region and the poisoned River that cuts right through it, to melt this woman's ears and eyes and glasses and face like tossing a candle into a swamp fire. I chew on the inside of my cheek until it bleeds, giving me a thoughtful expression as I devour my own flesh. Salt and copper. The AC shuts off, making it quieter than the presumed quiet was a second before.

Officer Man scans the report. "You had a direct line of fire, and refused to take the shot, later claiming that your magazine had jammed."

The AC shuts off again, in another office that's this exact office, letting loose the low rumble of moving water. I start to get dizzy, and grip the arms of the chair, trying to keep my organs straight up and down like they were in the waiting room.

Officer Massaquoi turns a page, the paper crackling in the ozone. "A Laotian militia found you wandering hundreds of miles from the nearest American front line. We assumed you went AWOL from your platoon, but we can't find you assigned to any active platoon, company, or battalion after your detainment at Quang Tri. You literally fell off the map of Southeast Asia nine weeks after landing here."

My head is buzzing. Something is trying to break through, riding the taste in my mouth into the outside world. Blood. Liquid moving very, very fast.

"Intercepted reports from the North Vietnamese active in western Laos near the DMZ discuss a victory over American forces on the Laotian side of the border. This isn't aircraft they're talking about, but boots on the ground. Soldiers. We assumed a rogue fire team. Hotshots who chased the NVA over the border and then ran into Tank Brigade 202. But we don't have any reports of this on our end. No missing soldiers, other than a few scattered throughout the country, and a few in the rear."

I know of five soldiers that went missing in the rear, plucked from holding cells and eternal KP duty and fake doctor's offices just like this one by a gray-eyed, blood-soaked angel of mercy, and then disappeared for good in the front where there weren't any lines. Medrano. Darby. McNulty. Render. Me.

"Your inactions led to the death of three good men," Officer Man says. "Good old American boys. Future leaders, masters of industry, not the rabble you run with."

I snap my attention to him, just like I did last time, but this time find Officer Massaquoi. The River keeps twisting.

"And then we find you," she went on, scowling. "On the far end of Laos, near death, presumed criminally derelict or perhaps on the run from a failed objective that has no record of existence in a country where we have no authorization to operate."

I'm following along with her words, mirroring them inside my mouth, knowing what she is going to say as she says it. *Déjà vu* of a *déjà vu*, spiraling down from the place where the new knowledge waits to reveal itself. Headwaters. The messages and the marching orders come to me from upstream, where the fire starts before it gently heads my way.

She holds up the orange again. It's just as round as her perfect little head. "When delivered to Udorn Air Force Base, you told your intake officer that you... How did you put it..." She holds up the paper to the lamplight on his desk and aims those reflective lenses at it. "'Peeled the skin off his head, off his face, like opening an orange.'" The lit glass circles return to me. "Do you remember doing this?"

"I do not, ma'am."

"Do you have anything to say for yourself?" he asks.

"I do not, sir."

"Do you think you're capable of such things?" she asks. "Doing what you said you did?"

"I do not, ma'am."

"Nothing," he says flatly. "Which is all you are. So much chaff for the mill."

"If you say so, sir," I say.

"And yet, you said it," she says.

"If you say so, ma'am," I say.

"You don't remember a good amount of very important things, do you?" Both of their voices now, layered in with that other voice, bringing it down an octave and giving it a tail of reverberation that fidgets across the floor.

"I don't know," I say to the pair of glasses, unsure of who I'm talking to, and not caring either way. I know how this turns out. "I told you...I told all of you. *They* told you, I haven't been sleeping very well. Sleeping much at all. I can't...I don't..." How does one explain this to a set of ears that can't possibly understand? A set of eyes that haven't seen anything like I've seen? "I can't." It's all I have. Language becomes worthless at a certain point, especially when I'd be doing this again.

"What were you doing in Laos?" Officer Massaquoi asks.

"I don't know."

"But you *do* know. Of course you do," Officer Man says.

"No, I truly don't." I don't. Not really. I have an idea, but I never really understood any of it. It was another man's dream that wasn't ever fully explained, and went sideways before any explanation of why could be offered.

"What was your mission? Who was your commanding officer?" She raises her voice. The pressure of the final quarter. There would be no overtime. Not for her, anyway.

I say nothing. Chapel's face strobes across the interior of my skull, bouncing off spongy gray matter and working its way down to my mouth, which I close. She and he and them all can go straight to hell. They wouldn't get at Chapel. None of them would. Not even me, and I wish I could, to ask him a great many things, probably at the end of a barrel.

Another long stare from those two shiny disks floating behind the lamp. "What are we going to do with you?" the jack-o-lantern says. I blink, and the face behind the glasses is male, Asian. I've never seen this man before. He nods and closes the file, saying something that sounds Chinese.

My eyes are drawn to the paperweight. That jellyfish stuck inside the glass, surrounded by air. Officer Massaquoi's gaze follows mine, then she stands up, pulling down her shirt and smoothing her tie.

"Wait right here," she says, walking briskly to the office door.

"Where are you going?"

Officer Man turns. He speaks with all of their voices. "To get you the help you need."

A figure exits into the hallway, closes the door and locks it from the outside, leaving behind a slight smell of perfume, or maybe cologne. And sweat. The AC kicks on again. The River below my feet is gone.

I pick up the paperweight and feel the weight of it in my hand. Artificial in its heaviness. The hardness of the glass. The pink creature inside looks like it's still alive, caught in the middle of a dance. The Chinese man is standing in front of me, next to the desk, wearing a white lab coat because that's what doctors are supposed to wear. There is brown medicine bottle in his hand, and fear in his eyes, trapped behind those lenses.

Less than a minute later, the outer door opens and Officer Massaquoi reenters her office, two MPs holding M-16s standing close behind her. The office is empty and still, aside from the fluttering of the curtains, letting in a humid breeze from the broken window behind it. The paperweight is gone.

## Chapter Seven

## Hard Like a Jellyfish

I run up the alleyway, stripping off my blood-splattered over shirt, shoving it down inside a sewer drain. The short-sleeve shirt underneath is clean, covered in flowers. A tourist disguise for an illegal import. It's dry as fresh laundry. I never break a sweat doing work anymore.

"Just because the jellyfish is soft, it is a mistake to assume it is harmless."
    This was my voice. He had no idea what I was saying. I didn't either. He had an excuse. But I did, too. That's what I tell myself each and every time.

I pass a man sprawled on the bricks, face up. Eyes open. Could be dead. Probably dead. Might have seen me. Will be dead soon either way.
    The thing isn't behind me. Not here. Still inside.
    Inside.
    What I did inside...
    I did it for *it*.
    That thing.
    That horrible thing.
    I don't know what that thing is but I really *do* know what that thing is.

Still inside.

Inside is where I did it.

It for it.

Pulled the weight from my pocket.

Gripped it like a baseball.

Aimed for the glasses, where the two lenses meet.

Buried it in the Chinese man's face.

It crumpled like a hollow egg.

Hand stuck inside the front of a man's head.

Didn't know a face was so fragile.

Nose and lips and eyebrows pushed in.

A jawbone grinning, because it knows the secret.

Eyeball fell onto the chair.

Felt brains on my fingers.

Wiped off a man's memories on the front of my shirt.

Set the paperweight on the edge of his desk.

A jellyfish still drowning inside glass.

Glass like water, bubbles like air.

Dancing.

Not dead yet.

It's not dead yet.

It is not inside anymore.

It is now behind me.

Following me into the floating city.

Following me ever since that day in the jungle.

Will follow me until I die.

And become not dead again.

With it forever more.

I break from the ally onto the crowded street and immediately eyes turn on me. I am used to this. My heart beats too fast. Need to check in, get paid, go home and stay up. Watch the corners of the room and fight when the time comes.

I walk deeper, deeper into the city that becomes unmoored from solid land and begins to drift, filthy water holding up the flowers and flesh floating on top.

Got to get paid. Got to fix myself right and get behind the sandbags, rifle at the ready, and scan the perimeter. Black Shuck comes in under the wires, just like they did.

## Chapter Eight

## Roman Candles

The trio of choppers hugged the top of the uneven tree line in single file, staying below the radar and moving fast enough that the SAMs would never be fired in time. The stuttered roar of their engines sets upon the silence of the lightless hills, echoing back from the sudden rocky peaks with a madman's cackle, and was gone just as the night shrank back, leaving everything uncertain in its wake.

The bay door was open and the airman who arrived with the chopper was manning his M-60, looking through polarized sunglasses at a black sky without sun, barrel pointed down into the void and the impression of trees cloaking the skin of the earth like fur. No cities or villages. This was a prehistoric darkness from a time before man mastered fire.

The five soldiers in the third helicopter sat in silence, each huddled low inside themselves, sorting through the recent past, maybe allowing themselves to reach back toward home, and all wondering what waited for them when the choppers touched down in a secret place never shared with them. They traveled on faith, in desperation, and with some queer sense of loyalty to an unknown father.

The emergence of flickering lights far in the distance caught Broussard's attention. The night sky to the east was cut by green tracers, perforating the air in a silent sway, seeking the out the roaring aircraft that descended from outer space to eat up their world.

"Free fireworks, y'all!" Darby shouted, the pierce of his voice through the monotone roar startling everyone. "Just like the Fourth of Ju-*ly!*"

The far horizon erupted in a line of orange as napalm coated the ground, incinerating everything for what was probably five hundred yards. Could have been inches or miles at this distance.

"Bring the smoke!" Darby howled. "Bring that holy smoke, you zoomie motherfuckers!"

The man's eyes lit up, feverish with the knowledge of what that fire was doing. Broussard imagined it himself, piecing together images of what he had seen already in this war, adding in snapshots like a slideshow. He tried to share in Darby's enthusiasm, in his pride for the military might of the country that sent them all here, but he couldn't. His stomach turned instead, which only made him sicker, this time with shame. Men like Darby were made for war, descending from a long line of men who set off into the unknown to find and make more of it, hoarding every inch of ground that was left behind them. Broussard wasn't one of those men, so he closed his eyes.

The jellied gasoline burned off, leaving a roiling cloud bank of smoke that blended back into the dark as the light below faded. The tracers were gone.

Darby howled like a wolf. The airman slid the door shut again and stared at Darby through his polarized glasses.

"It's a new world, brothers. A brave new world," Darby said. "Grab a gun or get the fuck out!"

# Chapter Nine

## The Floating City

I walk out of the storefront and enter the fast-moving current made by a stream of motorbikes and odors and noise. The now-familiar stew of fish sauce, cigarette smoke, and rotting garbage spills out of alleys with hoarse shouts and Hong Kong club music. The canals are choked with trash and human waste. The streets are filthy. And still they come, just like I did, pouring into the Klong Toey slums from failing farms in northeast Thailand to the buzzing hive of corrugated shacks and wet markets, working where they can find a need, making and selling whatever they can, including drugs to the tourists and flesh to everyone. A floating mass of pure, naked humanity, where anyone can hide.

In my pants pocket—lighter now, with the jellyfish gone—is the payment for the Chinese doctor job down on Yaowarat. A little cash and enough lightly bruised chemical agents to get me by until they think they'll need me again. They don't use me all the time, because I stand out. I'm "a blinking sign," as the ex-VC general turned drug smuggler noted through his sneering interpreter, flicking open his fingers over and over again. Not many of my kind in Bangkok. Not many of my kind anywhere on this fucking planet. Monster hunted by a monster. Drop of ink in the Yellow Sea. More like brown among brown, beans and rice and beans, but no one sees the world like that.

Just like so many of the residents, the heroin flows down into the city from the mountain country, too, turning dry and white in hidden labs dodging one American government agency while sending smoke signals to another, keeping an eye on the political winds but knowing that a customer will emerge from the skirts of Lady Liberty sooner or later. The amphetamines come from India and an unregulated factory pumping out the same sort of legally acceptable narcotics that would get you locked up if called by another name, or possessed by a different hand.

I'm fading, spent from the stress of the doctor job, and need to get back to the cave and measure up the right temperature screwball to calm my brain but keep me awake. Israel Broussard needs to take his medicine. That's how I live, and survive. Cotton in the ears, and toothpicks between my eyelids, just like in the cartoons. I'd lose my shit without this, and the Triad knows it. Evil motherfuckers. They know everything, down here anyway. More than the government, that's for sure. It pays to have eyes and ears among the people instead of inside clean glass buildings far removed from the realities of the world.

But they took me on when I was living in an alley, curling up between trash bags, slapping rats away from my sleeping face. Recruited *me*, instead of the other way around. These killers thought I was a killer, too. A great killer of men. Black American Killer GI, butcher of the yellow man. But I'm not black, I'm brown, and they aren't yellow, they're brown, and I'm not a killer but I've killed brown men, which made me a traitor. Maybe I was being paid for treason. Thirty pieces of silver by a number of different names.

These days I'll kill anyone, regardless of shade or hue. That's what Black Shuck has done to me. *How* he's done me. It's my real boss, that evil cosmic hound, not that tin-pot general, who's just a tool in the Great Machine. It's Black Shuck who turned me into the animal it used to be and maybe still wanted to be before crossing over and becoming something else. Echoes of a past life left after the transformation. Jealousy and yearning all at the same time. Animals breed animals even when the animal is no more. Don't need chickens or eggs in the place where it comes from. Maybe it's always been like this, and doesn't know any other way than waiting and tracking and pouncing. I don't know a motherfucking thing, other than the platoon of bugs crawling up inside my skin, and the terrible feeling that I might fall asleep standing up, and then face Black Shuck in the street, totally exposed, with plenty of tunnels down.

People give me room as I walk on my way, keeping the feet steady, the organs properly aligned. They know whom I am, most of them. They know what I do, and what I will do. To them, I'm just another imported killer. If they only knew the real score, that the only person I can't kill is myself, because I know where I'll go, and what will be waiting for me there. They'd understand, of course, because they know what else is out there, beyond the rotten water and decayed cement, past the jungle and heavy clouds always threatening rain. They know how other things pass over and take up residence here. I never did before, not being a churched-up boy and not allowed to go into the swamp where I would have learned all about what was really out there, but I sure as shit know now.

I'll live as long as I can, and do what I need to do in the meantime.

It's what animals do.

Survive.

It's what animals who have never been animals do.

Endure.

I turn on my homing beacon and follow the current flow back to my apartment, head down, weaving through groups of expats, squatters, and day workers gathered at sidewalk noodle stalls. Drinking beer and smoking cigarettes and talking shit while slapping down tiles in games of *tam cuc*. Even though they know me, no one looks at me down here. I never could figure out if that was natural or by design. Could have been orders from the Triad that always filtered down and out into the street, up into the ramshackle slums, and into the temples, police stations, and government offices. Maybe I was a ghost already and didn't know it, pantomiming a life to keep me from falling back into the void where it waited for me and me alone.

It didn't matter. What was real and what wasn't stopped having any meaning a long time ago. I didn't know shit other than needing to get back to my four walls, fill my own sandbags and dig my 40 by 40, because the mortars were coming, forming up in the corners by the ceiling and arcing down to my bed. "Tube!" they'd yell, when the shell left the cylinder in some secret mortar position. "Tube!"

I think of Black Shuck and cross my fingers. I've been among the Vietnamese long enough to know that it doesn't mean good luck.

# Chapter Ten

## The Mirage at the End of the World

With a controlled drop, the choppers shed altitude fast, handing it off to the slow rising sun as an even trade with the break of dawn over the eastern mountain range.

A layer of fog gathered below the clear brightening sky as the aircraft descended. Underneath the foam of mist, small points of white flames outlined a circular LZ large enough to accommodate the three helicopters.

The Chinook touched down first, coming to a soft landing inside the circle of C4 burning inside tin ration cans, joined by the two Hueys. Pilots and the five soldiers exited the aircraft as a crew of Hmong militia members emerged from the bushes, dressed in loose-fitting wool tunics and pants, stepping quickly in their tire-rubber sandals. They hauled long rolls of green netting and threw and draped it over the choppers, concealing the killer whale and its two identical escorts into shapeless lumps not much different from the landscape in less than a minute.

Broussard took in the base, which was entirely unlike the location they'd just left. Instead of being situated on a hilltop, it was cut out of a depression in the earth that resembled a crater left by a meteor impact a million years ago, poking a secret hole into the furred skin of the jungle. Trees rose up on all sides except to the south, where a vast granite cliff rose up through the fog and into the clear sky, absorbing heat from the rising sun the men couldn't see down in the mist. There were two bunkers overgrown with living vines and saplings, not cut branches. The larger of the two bristled with radio wires and UHF/VHF mast antennae surrounding a large metal dish painted matte black. No foxholes broke up the ground. No perimeter razor wire, machine gun positions, or artillery units. Whatever this place was obviously didn't fear attack or value a defensive posture other than remaining invisible from above. This wasn't a fire base. It was for something far different, and it had been here for a while.

"Where the sam fuck are we?" McNulty said, putting to particular word what everybody was thinking.

"Gentlemen."

The unfamiliar voice turned each head to discover a man walking from a doorway that seemed to materialize from the granite backdrop of the base. He was tall, farm-boy white, with shiny, almost playful gray eyes that added a youthful quality to the handsome collection of wrinkles etched deep by years of squinting into foreign suns. Eyes that took in too many secrets, which seemed to amuse and sadden him. His uniform was pressed olive drab, without patches or markings of any kind. The forearms poking from his tightly rolled sleeves were stained with a random smattering of old tattoos picked up at unpronounceable outposts before any of the men before him were born. Near his wrist, broad and faded green, was a silhouette of a raven.

The man stopped and clasped his hands behind his back. His expression was friendly, but grim. "Welcome to Echo Site 66."

The men exchanged glances.

"Where are we, sir?" Render said.

"We're exactly where we need to be, Sergeant Render. The true front line."

"Which is?" Darby said.

The man turned to Darby. "Which is, Private Darby, the Royal Kingdom of Laos."

The men looked at each other again, this time with expressions ranging from shock to fear.

Darby smiled, knocked his helmet back from his eyes. "Well, I'll be goddamned."

"Begging your pardon, sir," McNulty said to the man, a touch of a Chicago accent hardening all of his r's.

"Yes, Private Second Class McNulty?"

"Well, sir, we're not supposed to be out here. Sir."

"Is that right?"

"Uh, yes sir. I mean… Ain't we?"

"I have a secret to tell you. Can I trust you with a secret? Can I trust all of you?"

No one responded. You never trusted anyone in Vietnam, especially the ones who insisted on it.

The man nodded, sensing the mood. "I get it. Believe me, better than most. But let me tell you this, from someone who would know: Trust is important out here, on the true front line. It's probably *the* most important thing, aside from dry socks. We're all we have now. We're *it*." He let this linger, as much out of staging as out of necessity. "I apologize if that comes as a surprise, which I have no doubt it does, but in times of war, no situation is concrete, no tomorrow set in stone. The only certainty we have is in ourselves, and our devotion to one another in the service of a cause. Does this make sense?"

The men nodded, some in spite of themselves. What else were they going to do? They were way, way off the reservation, with no feasible means of getting back.

"So I ask, can I trust all of you? I'm not asking you to trust *me*, not yet. But can I trust you?"

"Yes sir," they all said in unison, with varying degrees of enthusiasm.

"That's good. That's what we need, as we go about our business." The man began to pace slowly, digging into his thoughts, stopping occasionally for emphasis. "You see, I'm in the business of secrets. It's what I was trained to do, and I'm just a byproduct of my environment, shaped on the anvil of experience and training. This *mission* and its conception is a byproduct of my environment. Do you understand?"

"Yes sir," Broussard said. He deeply understood the transformation of environment. It was what brought him across the ocean, and to stand in front of this man in an unmarked section of Laos.

"The secret I have to tell you is this: We *are* supposed to be here. We, meaning *us*." He gestured to everyone. "This squad. Us." He pointed out into the jungle, to the south. "*They* aren't supposed to be here. They. Them."

"Which way you pointing?" Darby asked.

"To the south, Private Darby, where our country has set up shop to build factories instead of finish lines. Long-term housing instead of forward operating bases deep within the heart of the enemy, to destroy their capacity to wage war and their will to continue. So the south, Private Darby. I'm pointing to the goddamn south."

Darby took a drag from his cigarette, nodded, and smiled. "That's what I figured."

Render looked at Broussard, who looked back at him, wide-eyed. Neither had ever heard any military man speak this way, and certainly not a white one. This was the kind of talk you'd hear from the Black Power brothers, late at night or away from the rest, when the smoke filled the air of the tent and the hooch was passed around. It was heresy, spoken by a commanding officer, and gave them all a jolt of adrenaline.

The man looked up at the sky, squinting at something the rest of the group couldn't see. "Let's take this inside, shall we?" He gestured to the bunker, and the men walked to it single file, just like good American soldiers.

## Chapter Eleven

## Public Toasts to Private Wars

Augie Chapel couldn't take his gray eyes off the wall. The men in front of it—stars gleaming on shoulders and bars weighing down chests, drinking and laughing like this was an oyster brunch at the Old Ebbitt Grill—held the life and usually the death of hundreds of thousands, potentially millions, in their hands, and Chapel couldn't stop staring at the wall behind them.

It wasn't the wall itself, but the Martinique wallpaper coating it. The pattern was a series of repeating banana leaves, gently rounded and loosely arranged, with space to move through and see through in between. Lots of white space to contrast with the vivid green spotted with yellow tuffs. Chapel had seen it before, in the Beverly Hills Hotel when he was meeting a Hollywood producer to advise on yet another ridiculous film about the whip-smart intelligence community foiling yet another plan by the Commies. It looked like the backdrop to a Bel Air garden party, not a jungle.

But this was Okinawa, the island nation conquered by the last great empire conquered by the Yanks, and this wallpaper was as non-native to this country as a Vietnamese jungle would be, or the men sitting in front of the sanitized representation of one. Brigadier, lieutenant, and major generals, mixed with admirals of the fleet, vice, and rear variety.

Ladder-climbing men of past wars and current politics who would never have to descend into the stinking, devil-haunted Indochinese wilderness where there was no repeated pattern, only chaos and waiting death and wet and rot and mud soaked in blood and soaking through sun-bleached boots to destroy feet and make the mere act of walking a living hell. No strategically placed white space to peer out onto the other side and the bright, clean salvation from the green hell. These red-faced, gossipy men would never be forced to experience how the Ong Thanh jungle smelled and the sounds it made when your ears were listening for any clue as to what your fate would be one second into the future. Their wars were different. Every war before this one was different. It demanded a special sort of thinking, and none of them had it.

These men didn't belong here, and neither did this wallpaper. Both were an abomination.

And yet Chapel couldn't stop staring at it. It fascinated him. A fascination with the abomination like Conrad wrote about. His heart of darkness lay in Africa, but there are many hearts beating inside many shades of darkness, and some blacker and colder than anything a writer could possibly conceive or, heaven forbid, personally experience and live to put down on paper.

"Augie, you grouchy sumbitch, you haven't even touched your drink."

Chapel looked at the man and his crew cut, the only thing that tied him to his soldiering days in the European theater, when he had done a good job, and had his heart in the right place. These days, his heart was descending into a pool of fat growing north from his belt line.

He placed his index finger on the side of his sweating glass of Irish whiskey, easy on the ice. The brigadier general snorted, shook his head, and downed his scotch, as if to show Chapel how it was done. Once the diapers come off for good, everything in a boy's life comes down to a dick-measuring contest until the day that boy dies.

The men resumed their conversation about women or baseball or some weird mixture of the two. He couldn't really follow it, especially since he'd noticed the wallpaper. He traced his finger around the top of his glass, feeling the coldness and the blunted edge smoothed out for his protection. Chapel wouldn't start drinking until he'd had his say, but that moment hadn't yet happened. He'd flown in to Kadena Air Base and walked along weirdly suburban, American-style sidewalks and carefully arranged city blocks to discuss strategy for the conflict in Vietnam with all the top brass, to offer his asymmetrical ideas to fight and win and most importantly end what had rapidly become an unorthodox war between a nation too powerful to do what it had to do and a populist insurgency that would do whatever it had to do to transform its own country. That was his specialty, and Chapel had honed his talents by fighting battles around the edges of wars and underneath the covers of nations. He was an alchemist tasked with fusing spycraft with battlefield machinery, and he was very good at what he did. That was why he was sitting at this table in Okinawa, sharing the same rarified air with men who outranked him by a measure of fleets and battalions. But so far, they were the only ones talking, shouting about body counts and media reports and political backchannel bullshit that had nothing to do with winning the war and everything to do with winning the public perception battle back in the States. With jockeying for the next promotion, the senate seat that waited for any war hero brave enough to mount a campaign. They were analyzing, adjudicating, and executing a war on ledger sheets while men were tearing each other to ribbons over five yards of jungle mud.

"Are we going to talk about winning this thing?"

Chapel wasn't even sure he said this out loud, because he'd been saying it inside his head for months, and probably years. But with the laughter silenced, and every shiny face at the table turned toward him, he knew it had finally passed his lips.

"What do you think we've been doing here the past three days?" A rear admiral spoke up. Chapel knew him a little bit. A decent guy, but severely lacking as a strategist. All of these men knew about fighting, and some of them knew about killing, but very few of them knew fuck-all about the delicate dance of war.

"You mean aside from grab-assing?" Chapel said.

There was a silence. Rank and pedigree narrowed eyes and raised noses. Chapel didn't care. He moved between the ranks, the military branches, like Fred Astaire stepping between raindrops. He didn't have much time for any of them aside from using them as rooks and bishops while lying in the cut like a queen.

"Yeah, aside from the grab-assing," the brigadier general said.

"Okay, aside from that, you've spent the last three days missing the goddamn point."

An Air Force general sighed, rolling his eyes to the ceiling. "What the fuck is he *doing* here, anyway?"

"You know what he's doing here," The brigadier general didn't need to drop the names Bill Lair and Ted Shackley, or mention Operation Momentum and the Raven Forward Air Controllers. Operation Palace Dog. Chapel was deep in with it all, and these secret operations in the Laotian wilderness were essential to fighting and killing the North Vietnamese in large numbers well away from established boundaries— and complicating strictures—of war.

"No, my question is *why* is he here?"

"You know the answer to that, too."

The man shook his head and brought his glass to his mouth like a pacifier. "Goddamn spooks."

Chapel smiled. Many of his colleagues hated that term. "Spooks." "Spooky." "The Spook Factory." Chapel loved it, because he knew what the power of that term meant. He knew what fear could do that a million bombs and a billion bullets never could. You terrify a man when the blood gets up, you don't have to break his nose, and risk breaking your own hand. A clean victory. Everyone wins when fear does the work.

"Okay, Chapel, you got all the answers." The brigadier general sat back in his chair, letting his middle-age paunch breathe a little. "What point are we missing?"

"How to end this war."

"How to *win* this war, you mean." Air Force again. They never could keep their goddamn mouths shut. First to talk, first to run to their flying machines and skedaddle the fuck out of Dodge.

"No one wins wars," Chapel said, not meaning it to sound so melodramatic, because he wasn't that kind of guy. Not usually, but these days he wasn't so sure anymore. "No one that matters."

"Okay, semantics, but I ain't playing. How do we win this war?"

"You win the war by winning the war. You don't win the war by merely fighting the war."

"Is he drunk?" Another USAF. They tended to stick together, Chapel mused. "I haven't seen him drink much, but is he drunk?"

"Nah, he always talks like that," the Brigadier General said.

The man got to his feet. "Jesus H Christ. I'm taking a squirt."

"No, you'll want to stay for this, General. I mean, if you want to end the war."

"We ain't here to *end* any war. We're here to win it, or nothing."

"You have the first part right. You're not here to win this war. You're here to fight it, yes. You've shown the willingness to go all in on fighting it—well, *mostly* in—earning your paycheck, giving your job meaning, and your orders the weight of history being written with each signature. But winning it? What would be the point? What would all of you do if there was no war to fight?"

"You're talking like an asshole."

"He's talking like a longhair."

"Does longhair mean faggot?"

Chapel stared at the man, making a mental map of each lethal entry point that would kill him with a deftly applied salad fork.

"What do you suggest, Augie?" asked the brigadier general.

He was a good guy. Brave in battle. Thoughtful behind a desk. Always measured. Unfortunately, one is judged by the company they keep, and in this case…

"We make them not want to fight."

"We talking leaflets here? Leaflets *again*? Spook radio? A game of telephone?"

Snorts from the men.

"How would we do this?" The brigadier general hadn't taken his eyes off of Chapel. He knew him well enough to know when he was just spitballing and when he was bloodhounding.

"What do you think we're doing?" a new voice interrupted. Assistant Commandant of the Marine Corps. A real hard ass who wasn't good at politics, but played it anyway because he was too old to fight and it sure beat golf. "We'll killing them by the truckload every single goddamn day. Hell, we greased 75,000 the Easter Offensive, in case you haven't heard out in that campsite of yours."

"Yes, I've heard. I've heard a lot. Seen a lot, too. More than you probably know. You're killing them. Yes, indeedy and you betcha. Killing a lot of them, although not as many as you might think, what with the game of telephone that takes place for confirmed and probables. But we are killing a lot. Sure enough. Look at Laos, where all of this started anyway. We're on track to drop two million pounds of ordnance by the end of next year. A half a million sorties, gentlemen. A half a goddamn million. We've dropped more bombs on Laotian real estate per capita than any other nation in the history of this planet, and the Pathet Lao are still running free, hosting a VC boom-boom party and enough resupply lines along the Ho Chi Minh to arm up Charlie until the year 2000. We literally cannot drop more bombs and kill any more people than we already are, and where has it gotten us?"

"We ain't done shit in Laos," the assistant commandant said.

Most of the table chuckled, raised eyebrows and exchanged glances, except for the old marine and Chapel.

"You're not in front of a microphone, sir. We all know the score here."

"Do we?" he snorted. "Do we all know the score, because it seems to me that you're looking at the wrong fucking scoreboard."

"Scoreboards lie. Stat sheets lie. I'm looking at the play on the field."

"Then what's the problem? You losing your spine?"

Marines hated spooks most of all. First in, last to leave didn't have much time for those who skulked in the shadows. Chapel expected it, but the dig at his bravery did raise his normally rock-solid heart rate a few beats. Still, he kept his voice even and unchanged when he continued. "I have no problem with killing men, killing people. I've done it plenty, from miles away, and just a few inches. I know you have too."

"Yes, I have."

"It's unpleasant, isn't it?"

"Depends."

"Yes, it always depends. That great rolling wave of ethical morality."

"Augie."

Chapel turned to the brigadier general.

"How do we make them not want to fight?" he asked.

"We scare them."

"Pardon?"

"We scare them." More chuckles from the table, draining away the tension in the air and rebuilding every defensive bunker each man brought to the officer's club that day. Some outright laughed, checking out of the conversation. Chapel was used to this, too, so he pressed on. "Not with cluster bombs. Not with dead bodies, or even atrocities. We've done all that, and what has it gotten us? No, we go deeper. We get into the core of each man, woman, and child fighting for the Communist cause, and we scare the living daylights out of them."

The brigadier general was still listening, as was the old marine.

"You can't kill an idea. You can't kill a person enough to change their mind."

"Worked on the Germans," the marine said.

"And the Japanese," the brigadier general said, his eyes following their waiter, who couldn't hide his glance at the table as he walked past.

"That was different. They were fighting for a country, the idea of a country ruled by a supreme leader that offed himself in one case and was castrated by two mushroom clouds in the second. It was all gone, the dream was over, the supremacy was a sham, the armies were decimated, so they gave up. Now out there," Chapel pointed to the southwest, not at the god awful wallpaper, "in Vietnam, fed by the surrounding regions of sympathetic support, they're fighting for an *idea*. We'll never take their country, seize their land. We're not here for that. Don't have the capability, nor the desire, and they know this. We want to break them, shatter their will, not colonize and exploit."

A few of the brass had excused themselves, but a few had stayed, and they weren't laughing anymore.

"They own the countryside," Chapel continued, "and always will, so they're fighting and willing to die for an idea, a belief that approaches the religious. This is just another stage in their drawn-out independence day, from the French, from an aristocracy and government in bed with every new-style colonizer that doesn't give a good goddamn about the rice farmer stepping through buffalo shit in the Mekong Delta. We'll never bomb or shoot that out of them. We'll have to kill every single North Vietnamese, Viet Cong, and ICP sympathizer in the country. The British couldn't do it to us, so why do we think we can with them?"

"Give us enough time," the marine said, "and we will."

"No, you won't. You can't. It's impossible. So the war will never be won, and because of that, without us declaring defeat, it'll never end. We'll be throwing our boys into the meat grinder from now until the Rapture."

"The United States doesn't lose wars," said a new voice, an army four star.

"It does now. It is every day. Don't believe what you read in the papers. I know you have better intel than that. We're losing this war, and allowing it to happen."

"That sounds real close to treason," the army general said.

Chapel jabbed his finger into the table, his blood up. "I love my country. I'd die for my country and I'll probably get the chance. I love it so much that I don't want to see it lose any more of its sons on a war that can't be won, and won't be won, not the way we're now doing it. We need to rethink the whole thing, from the top down. Go asymmetrical, fight sideways and upside down, just like they do, but do it our way. Take our tactics from the secret war and institute them country-wide. Get weird, dig down into the myths and gods and spirit realm and fuck with their heads, because we sure as hell aren't fucking with their hearts. It's the only way we win."

There was silence, stunned and otherwise.

"I'm talking a piss." The four star got up from the table so abruptly that his chair fell backward onto the floor. "Oh," he added over his shoulder. "And fuck you, Chapel."

The rest of the group was glaring at him, disgust and something worse breaking through the blear of bloodshot eyes, except for the assistant commandant and the brigadier general.

"Major, I think it's time for you to leave."

"You haven't even heard my idea."

The brigadier general got to his feet and put his hand on Chapel's shoulder. It was friendly, but had a little extra heat in the grip. "We've heard enough ideas for one day."

Chapel looked at each face in turn of those who remained at the table. These were the men tasked with managing this war. Not fighting it like the Vikings fought or the Trojans fought or the Zulus fought or the Lakota fought or the Army of North Vietnam fought, but managing it, and they couldn't even call it what it was, let alone win the goddamn thing.

Either all-in, by whatever means, or go the fuck home. No one at this table was all-in anything except their third bottle of Johnnie Walker and fifth trip to the bathroom. It was a travesty. It was an abomination, every bit as much as that fucking Martinique wallpaper. The stand-in jungle for the stand-in leadership, starting with Nixon and Westmoreland and traveling on down, like shit dropped on a dusty red hillside.

He moved his gaze back to the wallpaper, where the four star was talking to an aide, gesturing in his direction.

Chapel dropped his white handkerchief onto his uneaten plate of food and rose from his seat. "Listen up, Little Foxes. There are people who eat the earth and eat all the people on it, and other people who just stand around and watch them do it."

He walked out of the officers' club, disappearing into the shadows like the spook he was and would always be. Not one pair of eyes watched him go.

## Chapter Twelve

## Poison in the Hangar

Chapel strode across the tarmac, frustrated, furious, cursing the bloodline of each red face at that table in four different languages. Sometimes English just didn't take you to the right place.

A blaring horn stopped him short, saving him from walking nose-first into a friendly-fire death under the wheels of a convoy. Chapel's maledictions were drowned out by the chug of engines as transport trucks rumbled by, beds full of barrels stamped MONSANTO and painted with a bright orange band, the agrichemical razor blade sent from a factory in Grand Island, Nebraska, to shave off the hiding spots of the entire North Vietnamese Army and any other creature that dared shrug at the national anthem. They'd been dumping this stuff on the country for years, and they'd keep right on until the entire subcontinent was a desolate wasteland of mud and sticks. And they still wouldn't have won the war, which would just go deeper underground.

Chapel watched the last truck disappear into a hangar, and the door shut behind it. He stood that way for a long time, taking measure of the building and what was housed inside it. So many barrels. Enough to last a lifetime.

The rage that had been playing with the lines on his face altered, shifting into the more familiar sketches of grim determination, lit by the wonder of possibility that forever played in those shiny gray eyes.

Chapel began to walk again, this time almost jogging, formulating a flow chart of every favor owed to him in every branch of the military and intelligence service from Da Nang to DC. His loose pockets were filled with chits that he'd cash in at a dozen tellers. Nothing was out of reach if you knew who to ask, and how. Thirty years of bootlegging built up quite the black book.

By the time he reached his chartered Beechcraft, the formula was worked out. Chapel was going to end this war.

## Chapter Thirteen

## The Nightmare Factory

The inside of the bunker was surprisingly spacious and dry, even comfortable, in the minimalist style of a monastery. The floor was lower than the outside ground, carved out of the stone and squared off in the corners. The furniture was functional but fine, showing strength in complement to taste. A sturdy mahogany table was littered with maps, data sheets, various odd pieces of equipment, and books on Vietnamese history, folklore, and religion. Oil lanterns burned, which cast everything in a warm yellow glow. The room looked more like long-term living quarters for an overly organized eccentric than a temporary field office for the U.S. military.

Chapel stood behind the table and regarded each man in turn, looking them up and down and lingering on their faces, probing their eyes. "It's good to see you all at last, in the flesh."

The men glanced at each other. Everyone was at a loss for words.

"My name is Augustus Cornwallis Chapel, but everyone in the outside world calls me Augie. But we aren't in the outside world, are we? Pretty goddamn far from it, so you can call me Chapel. My rank isn't important. Hasn't been important for a long time. So Chapel it is. The man behind me to my right—" He cocked his head in that direction to a tall, lean man wearing headphones adjusting the controls of a reel-to-reel playback device mounted on a wheeled cart. "—is Morganfield." Morganfield nodded to the men as Chapel continued. "That's not his real name, so don't bother looking it up when you get back to Boise or Des Moines, because it doesn't exist. I did this for his protection, but I am most definitely Augustus Cornwallis Chapel, because I need no protection." He gestured to the chairs arranged around the table. "Now that introductions are out of the way, please, have a seat."

The men sat down, joined by Morganfield. Chapel remained standing.

"I'm sure you all have many questions," Chapel said, "and I will answer all of them in due course. But first, please allow me to explain why you are all here."

"Sir?"

"Specialist Broussard."

"I don't mean to interrupt, but…" Broussard hesitated, not sure if he should continue.

"Speak freely."

"Well, sir, what's been bothering me since I arrived at base camp is, well, this team doesn't make sense."

"Is that right?"

"Yeah, I mean, this isn't your normal fire team, is it? Render's a Marine. Darby, too. McNulty, Medrano, and I are Army. I don't know who or what Morganfield is, but he looks like Air Force."

The men laughed. Chapel smiled and crossed his arms. "He is most definitely *not* Air Force."

"So, how did we all get here? Together, I mean."

"I chose you. All of you." Chapel's eyes moved across each of the men. "You were selected."

"But why?"

A smile played across Chapel's lips. A grunt who needed to know why raised the dander of any officer, but Chapel also appreciated a soldier who took the risk to question, to judge motives, looking for truth and suspicious of abuse of power. He was the same sort of grunt, way back when. "Because I believe in second chances," Chapel said. "Third and fourth, even, in the case of Lance Corporal Darby."

More laughter.

"Hey, for that third one, I was framed."

"But I'm also a pragmatist," Chapel continued, "and I'm selfish, and I want to execute this mission, on my terms, with no outside interference. To do so, I needed good soldiers who stumbled and were cast aside, declared unfit for combat, when nothing could be further from the truth."

Broussard thought about that night, the two a.m. perimeter rush by the VC at Hill 407 when he didn't take the shot from the lip of his foxhole, his muscle memory of how to pull the trigger when he was commanded failing him utterly, the ignorant flesh seizing up and shutting down, leaving his brain in charge. His brain told him to close his eyes, curl up and not draw attention with a muzzle flash. The brain decided to protect the body, to keep it going to accomplish its genetic imperative of replicating itself instead of this secondary mission of killing another human or many humans, denying them their right to endow their genetic code to the greater species. His brain hoped they'd all pass right over him, each sandaled foot and grunting body; that it all would go away and the world would return to normal. That somehow he'd be back in the bayou, lying in tall, hot grass of his grandmother's back yard, the wet blades itching his skin, listening to the insects whisper secrets to each other. He wasn't a killer, and didn't know how to be. There was no light switch on the back of his head to flip from one who was embarrassed to hit a boy on the playground to one who could kill a complete stranger in the pitch blackness of two a.m. He didn't know how to negotiate that in his mind, didn't have enough time to travel to that new destination in his soul. The muscle training and mental reprogramming of boot camp didn't get him there, nor did humping uniform and rifle and his terror through the jungle, being eaten alive by mosquitoes and leeches and jumping at every sound that didn't seem to come from the sky or the trees, knowing that each moment could be his last. And the insects sounded different here. Alien. The birds, too. All of it was wrong, and he had wanted it to just go away but it didn't, even when the gunfire ended and he was dragged from his foxhole by his lieutenant, screaming into his face and spitting on the ground. No one in his platoon would look at him. He hadn't even be in-country long enough to learn anyone's name.

No one died for what he did, or more rightly, what he didn't do, but they could have. After pulling him from the ground, his lieutenant had kicked him out of the bush and sent his ass back to Quang Tri to await a transfer and possible charges. He'd sat in a chair then, too, but his eyes hadn't changed. Not yet. They were the same ones he always had, weak and half blind and in need of correction. He sat with himself and those memories of Hill 407, wishing he could do it all over but afraid that it would turn out the same way. It was the first time since he was ten that he wanted to kill himself, and set his brain to that while his muscles claimed amnesia regarding that last night in the jungle. That was when the note came, the doors swung open, a jeep waiting for him outside. His bootlaces were in his hand, the pipe above him already picked out.

"Each of you became an 'issue' to your commanding officers," Chapel continued, "and were removed from your platoons or squads and set up to disappear inside the belly of the United States military, which is where I came in. I found you all, and brought all here, for that last shot at honor. In this theater, anyway."

Broussard looked at Chapel, the man who had saved his life. Chapel returned his gaze with those shiny gray eyes, the slightest hint of a wry grin twisting itself across his face again. Broussard wondered if he knew. Somehow, he was confident that he did, but also didn't consider it worthy of any special notice. He probably did things like that all the time.

Habitual heroism.

"How?" Medrano asked. "How'd you come in? I mean—" he gestured around the bunker—"this don't exactly look like it's on the books, know what I mean?" The men were loosening up, realizing that this wasn't a normal military situation, and that communication was more of a two-way affair.

"Never ask a girl her secrets, Private Medrano." Chapel said, eyes winking without the lids ever closing. The soldiers laughed, loosening up. Some men were just born with that natural way.

Chapel opened up a leather case from the table and took from it a worn corncob pipe that was surely made a century or two prior. He held onto the pipe as he addressed the group.

"Gentlemen, I've brought all of you to this place for what I see as a very important reason. The United States government might not necessarily agree with me, but I felt the need to call an audible here, and check down into a new play after surveying the defensive alignment. Do we understand each other?"

"Yes sir," four of the men said in unison.

Medrano looked puzzled. McNulty cuffed his arm. "Football, dummy."

"That's good," Chapel said. "We need to understand each other, now and for the duration of this specialized commission, and even afterwards. An understanding, and a trust, will be important to successfully see this through. Can I count on you?"

"Yes sir," all of them said.

Chapel nodded and leaned forward, hands gripping the edges of the table, like a professor in lecture. "The situation is this: We're only officially fighting Charlie on one side of a border that is invisible to our enemy, allowing the Ho Chi Minh Trail cut through the mountains of Laos to act as a greased conduit to move farm-fresh troops, extract casualties, and resupply all manner of warm and fuzzy weaponry gifted by our friends the Chinese. These weapons are killing our brothers in record numbers up and down this confused nation we have pledged our lives to cleanse of the insidious virus of Communism. We cannot allow this to go on."

"No sir," McNulty said, a weird grin on his face. The true believer, zealot of any religion that allowed him to wage war against the Other. Chapel was just the latest prophet. Lord willing, there'd be more.

"No sir, indeed." Chapel carefully unwrapped a cloth covering a tightly wound braid of tobacco, its spicy musk cutting through the humid air. "In a war, if the enemy leaves the battlefield and retreats to the village, you chase him to the village. If the enemy runs to a church, you pursue him into that church. If the enemy runs across borders, we cross those borders to defeat our enemy, politicians and gold stars be damned."

"Goddamn them anyway," Render said.

Chapel opened a bowie knife, its long, fat blade catching the lantern light. "We will chase our enemy to their village, to their church. We will go where they go to hide, to heal, and to rest, and we will roust them from their beds." He lowered the knife to the table and carefully cut the tobacco. "That is what brings us here, away from the politicians and the gold stars, and the platoon commanders who follow them like good soldiers. I don't blame them, but I also don't cut smoke for them, for they're not the brothers I need." He picked up a plug of tobacco and brought it to his nose, closing his eyes and inhaling deeply. Chapel opened his eyes and held up the moist brown leaf. "But you are the brothers I need."

The men stared up at him. He was speaking a language that they never knew existed, but always craved. It was nourishment to a group of souls that had been starved of respect since their first day in the service and much further back than that, and they ate it up.

Chapel placed the tobacco into the bowl of the pipe and slowly packed it with a pewter tamper. "All of our best efforts at fighting this enemy with one arm tied behind our backs have failed. We kill them in one country, and they reconstitute in another, like some goddamn supernatural entity.

So I've decided to take the fight to them, where they rise again from the dead. I know where they do this, as I have many eyes that see many things, and we will hit them one by one, in this country that's older than time, that's laughed at a hundred armies throughout history, and lately at a thousand tons of American ordnance. Uncle Sam will not be laughed at. Our ego cannot take it. As such, creative measures must be taken. That's where we come in. *We* are the creative measure."

The older man looked at the younger ones sitting in front of him, hearts as open as their mouths. He understood humanity, even if he didn't like it much anymore. But that keen understanding of how it ticked was why he was so good at what he did, and why what he was about to do would certainly work.

Chapel held up the loaded pipe. "In this pipe I have placed the best Carolina tobacco ever grown. It was first planted by slaves for their white masters. Out here, in this new world we've ripped apart by the seams, there are no slaves and no masters. We are all both. Slaves to fire and to death. Masters of fire and of death. We serve and command both. That is the nature of what we do, this business of war."

Chapel struck a wooden match with his thumbnail, put the flame to the pipe and inhaled deeply as the bowl glowed orange. He blew out a small cloud of pure white smoke.

"We will smoke this tobacco, all of us, as this is a pipe of war, carved by my grandfather just before he went into battle against his own countrymen." He took another drag, and the smoke billowed, slow and coiling, pulling the words out of his mouth. "The First Tribes smoked pipes as symbols of peace, but we are a different breed. We are dogs of war."

He passed the pipe to Medrano, who inhaled deeply, expecting a cough as he blew out. Instead, he raised his eyebrows and smiled, passing the pipe to Render.

"I've read all of your files, from cover to cover," Chapel continued. "But even then, I don't know you. And lord knows you don't know me, where I've been and what I've done, and I'm okay with that. But know that whatever you see, and whatever you hear, out in the jungle once we're activated, trust me that I'll see you through. I'll bring you back in one piece, sound of body, and sound of mind, even if things get weird, and they *will* get weird."

The pipe had moved on through Render and McNulty to Darby, who took an extra hit, and then to Broussard, who wiped off the stem and put it to his lips, sucking in air and bringing red life to the packed leaf under the ash. His lungs filled with hot, spicy smoke, making him dizzy as he passed it back to Chapel.

"We are messengers, gentleman, and we will deliver a message of strange vengeance to a very determined enemy that does not respect us, but is more that capable of fearing us." Chapel inhaled deeply from the pipe, smoke billowing out from his lungs as he spoke like a pale dragon. "We will deliver to them the Fear, upon wings of sharpened steel. We have not earned his respect, this enemy in the jungle, and never will, but we will give him the Fear, pulled from the deepest part of his soul."

Chapel stretched out his arms, indicating the bunker, filled with odd equipment and lined with radar and that strange audio equipment. "Witness the nightmare factory, gentleman. You are all now part of Operation Algernon."

## Chapter Fourteen

## Sleeping in the Temple of Mars

That night, the five bedded down in a high-ceilinged tent next to the bunker, lying in sturdy cots with thick, clean blankets that smelled of pine crates instead of sweat, mud, and shit. There were no mosquitoes here, as if they feared disturbing this incongruous sanctity of secrets. The war sounded far away, coming to them as muffled thuds of heavy bombs far in the distance, with none of the close-by chatter of machine guns. In the relative silence, none of them slept, except for Darby, who snored to the ceiling, mouth wide enough to let in all manner of spider, if they were more heretical than the mosquitoes. One mission was the same as another to Darby. He was there to kill people as directed, and would do so when called up, and sometimes when he wasn't, which was what brought him into the group.

"What was he talking about, the Fear?" Medrano whispered, mostly to himself, but loud enough the rest of the men could hear. "Nightmares and stuff. Operation Ala-non."

"Algernon," Broussard said. "Like the writer."

"Which one?" Medrano said.

"Can you talk in your sleep with your mouth shut?" McNulty said, fighting with his pillow, the quiet creeping into his brain and waking up things the noise usually kept down.

"What do you think we're doing out here?" Medrano said, eyes darting back and forth in agitated thought.

"Does it matter?" Render said.

"Of course it matters, man," McNulty said, sitting up. "This guy could be fucking crazy."

"All white people are crazy," Render said, sounding tired.

"Hey!" said McNulty. "Present company included?"

"Most definitely," Render said. He didn't want to explain his entire conscious life to a guy who would never understand it anyway.

"Well, fuck you too," McNulty said, jamming his head back onto his pillow.

"He ain't crazy," Broussard said.

Everyone waited for Broussard to continue, but he didn't.

"How do you know?" Medrano said.

"His eyes."

Broussard rolled over.

"What kind of fucking answer is that?" McNulty said.

He received no reply.

Now it was McNulty's turn to sigh and roll over, which he did with big, frustrated moves. "Man, you fucking people."

In the dark, Broussard and Render opened their eyes, sharing a look without even seeing each other. Medrano closed his and groaned. Darby snored through it all.

## Chapter Fifteen

### Beast at Bay

Another chair.

My life, this life, now,

spent in a series of chairs.

Waiting.

To kill or be killed.

To be told that you're sick or that you're a coward or that you're going to be locked in a cage as a sick fucking coward.

Throw away the key.

Throw away the chairs.

Sitting here, sitting there, sitting and waiting in a fucking chair.

Becoming the chair.

Stiff, unwieldy.

Four legs and two arms.

One back.

Body of a beast with the arms of a man.

Fucking werewolf caught in transformation and stuffed and stuck in a museum of horrors.

Or a rich man's den.

Same thing, sometimes.

Sometimes.

I'm not going to move from this chair.

Something heavy impacts the inside of the wall.

For eighteen hours I've sat in this chair. It's the only one I own, the only piece of furniture in the cave aside from that gruesome bed. That coffin floating on water.

I found the chair broken and rotting in the back alley of a shooting gallery, just like I was when they found my busted ass, broke ass, and knew it had to go home with me.

I sit in this chair because it isn't comfortable, and is a place to fix up and then rest between hours of pacing. It's not conducive to sleep, or anything other than sitting uncomfortably and keeping watch.

Two arms and four legs. Those four legs.

Black Shuck has been waiting behind the wall for eighteen hours, patient as a dead moon, looking for its way in.

I'm not letting it, and I can feel its rage.

A huge snout sniffs frantically in the corner of the room where the wall meets the ceiling like a panting dog on the spoor.

I remembered my Zora like others do Sunday school lessons, worming its way through all those shut doors and broken hallways to sit with me on the front porch. "Whut's de mattah, ol' Satan, you ain't kickin' up yo' racket?" My God, was she my religion.

A whine comes from behind the wall. It's a strange sound coming from what it comes from, filled with frustration.

"Fuck that old hound," I say aloud, just to make sure I'm still real, that the room is the cave and isn't a prison or the box inside my mind that closes on top of me. I repeat it, my voice sounding strange to my own ears.

"Fuck that old hound… Fuck that old hound…"

I keep this up for hours, until my voice goes hoarse.

Something heavy impacts the inside of the wall.

"Why do we scrap?" I say, tongue brittle as paper. "Why do we scrap, old hound?"

A small scratching sound comes from inside the wall. Slow and deliberate. Bits of metal pulled from brutalized bodies. Claws from an impossible beast.

"I don't need your land, and you don't need mine."

The scratching stops.

"You stay where you are, and I'll stay where I am. Everything'll be cool."

Something shifts inside the wall, pushing it outward, cracking the plaster from ceiling to floor.

"Put away your claws, and I'll put away mine."

Silence.

"We'll leave each other alone."

Silence.

"We were born to breed, to eat, and to run free. Each and all of us."

The scratching sounds begin again, this time forceful, frenzied. Determined.

"We weren't born to war, but war is what we made."

The wall plaster buckles, pieces falling to the clean cement floor.

"Why do we scrap, old hound?"

A furred black paw pushes through the wall. I get to my feet as the chair splits and falls behind me. My hands ball into fists, my own claws dig into my palms, dripping blood onto the tops of my bare feet.

"Because we're all fucking animals," I sneer behind clenched teeth. "Me and you and you and me."

The wall explodes outward into the room, chunks of moldering plaster and cheap lath skittering across the floor, pushed by a cloud of dust that billows like smoke.

"Fuck you, old hound. You ain't nothing but a goddamn dog."

The dust clears and Black Shuck stands before me, an obsidian boulder parting the cloud of dust swirling around bunched muscles and corded sinew. I can see it now. Now, I see the hound, and it's terrible. But not as terrible as me.

"And I'm a fucking dragon."

---

I open my mouth to breath fire, and Black Shuck opens jaws of its own. We run at each other, but my mouth can't open wide enough, and its maw gets so much bigger. So, so much bigger. An eternity of black opening up in front of me. Things swirl inside that mouth, twisting down its throat. Galaxies, nebulae, all sucked into a slowly spinning black hole that roars in reverse, so slow and low it means to rip apart every tiny building block inside me.

Black Shuck snaps shut its jaws and all goes black. I am either asleep, or I am dead. Unmade. Stardust once more.

I'm diving into the swimming hole, the water taking my ten-year-old body in and hugging me tight as I glide through the murk, bringing me back to the surface before I even need to take a breath. Treading water, I wipe water from my eyes and turn back to the dock, where my brother stands, uncertain, bones quivering inside his skinny frame. Knees turning in on each other. I mock him. Me, the brave boy not afraid of the water. The hero who knows how to float.

He turns to leave, to get his towel and his shoes and head home, but I say something that turns him back around, to face me and the water. I say it again, because we're alone, and I know exactly where to go inside him to find what I need.

His bones are no longer quivering, and his knees are straight. With an expression on his face that I'd never seen before, he steps off the dock and knifes into the water, feet-first. He sinks like a stone, and just like a stone, he doesn't float back to the surface. Not until much, much later.

I wake up in darkness with a bag over my head, drawstring cinched tight around my neck. The inside of the bag is olive-green and is trying to eat through my scalp, chewing through hair and licking at my skin. Black Shuck is inside the bag, shrunk down but with the same teeth and rotten breath smelling like an east Texas feedlot.

My fingers claw at the strings around my neck and find that they aren't there anymore, then rip off the olive-green boonie hat and throw it across the room. Black Shuck roars from inside the bush hat, its wrinkled green dog house, and I push open the door and flee the cave, needing to move my spider limbs, put some blood back into my extremities and get away from the River where my brother sank, that keeps pulling me back into its waters where I once floated like I invented the whole world. And I don't want to sit in the chair and look at the wall anymore and feel the presence of the boonie hat and think about what's inside of it, hidden by one fold that no one ever thought to open.

And I need a drink.

I'm strung out, worse than ever, the opium dragging me to sleep in the chair while the Dexedrine waits to fry my nerves when I wake up, if I can even tell the difference between the two. Waking or asleep. Live or dead. All too real or just one big fucking fake. I can't take it anymore. I'm near the edge, and that's a dangerous place. I could fall, right down the million-mile throat into the black hole belly of a hound.

I'm awake now, I think, and on the move, slicing through crowds that part before my blade. Have to walk off the shakes, and get a drink or two or seven in me to keep my mind together and move me back from the cliff.

Human contact. I despise it, fear it, but I know that I need it right now. Right now, after nights or days or days of nights like these, when the hound finds its way in while my eyes are still open and some of those doors threaten to open wide. I need to get away from the River. All of them, and everything that waits for me under the water, accusing me with wide open eyes.

Cut this crowd, feet moving like a fly to dead flesh. Had to get out of the cave. The water. Sleep is strongest in an empty room. So is madness, and so is Black Shuck. It wouldn't dare touch me in a crowd. At least it hadn't yet. Times can and do change. The gaping hole in my wall was testament to that.

The floor was wet when I left, and I needed dry land.

## Chapter Sixteen

## The Last Chance Saloon

I readjust my hips in the booth, sore from the chair and getting eaten. I sip my drink, Irish whiskey with a splash of good Javan coffee. No ice cubes, because Bangkok doesn't do ice cubes, not even in the upscale hotels. Fuck what the tourists want because what they want rarely involves ice cubes.

The place is crowded, but it could be just me unable to mentally navigate groups of people until I get this first drink down. I don't stand out here as much, sometimes being mistaken for a tourist by the new bar girls and some of the freshly deposited expats. Burned-out hippies, most of them, a few Australians on holiday, but also some real hard chargers, who want to burn their candle down to ash in the new Old West buried in one of the oldest spots in the east. They all hit me up for drugs and tips on the best brothels or sex clubs or places where men can rent village boys by the hour. One look from my eyes so new and different from theirs, that have seen the jungle and what lies beyond, usually sends them down the bar, but some of them stick around long enough to buy me a drink and endure ten minutes of strained silence. Either way, it's a free drink for a man perpetually on a budget.

I look around the room, getting a temperature reading for the crowd tonight, looking for shadows in the corners. Nothing but the usual scene, for the most part. A bit of an edge in the air, or maybe that's just my veins bulging under my skin, locked in the confused struggle of needing to purge narcotics while at the same time trying to conserve every bit of them.

A loud voice erupts from the front of the bar, the place with the most visibility, and vulnerability. I can't understand what he's saying, but the gibberish is most definitely English, mashed flat by the landscape of the Middle West.

Now that I know the score, my ears can't help but comb through the background noise and braid his voice into words.

"…greased three gooners all by myself. Sure as shit did."

He's the right age, but isn't the right type. He's wearing a black beret, checkered black and white VC scarf around his neck, and a khaki safari shirt, all of them props from entirely different plays. New combat boots on his feet without a scuff on them, down below shorts held up by a brown dress belt. Fat legs. A face that hasn't seen anything but the inside of a cheeseburger bag and too many matinees. No one who did what we did would talk this way, not in mixed company, in that tone of voice. Maybe I'll let him wear my boonie hat for a while and see how he makes out with that.

"Four shots, three stuffed body bags," this cheeseburger went on. "If those dirty bastards used them, which they didn't. Just dragged them back into the jungle or God knows where else."

The Vietnamese in the bar, and there aren't many but enough, cast their glares on the man and his entourage of imports and locals of several genders. Bar girls, lady boys, sleaze tourists, and a Eurotrash couple ogling the king shit of Ugly America.

"You ever see the insides of a man? No, *no*… No women. What do you think I am, an animal? Warrior's code, ladies and gentlemen and lady gentlemen."

Laughter. Some applause. Fucking applause. Could be a diplomat or a businessman, special attaché or some shit like that, but I smell the stink of the long con all the way across the room.

"War is hell, know what I'm saying? And it was a hell of a party. Can we drink to that? I think it's only right."

They do, because apparently it is.

This man is embarrassing me, playing the part of one of my own but he most certainly is not. He's shaming those slow dying deep roots, trained for drought and stubborn as weeds.

My feet move before my brain can tell them not to. The transplant Vietnamese, a lot of them veterans, won't say anything. They have too much class. But I will. I'm a veteran, too, and I lost my class a long time ago.

I stand behind the guy and look down at him, see the shoe polish collecting around the fat behind his neck. Unless he was a general, this turkey is too old to have been there with us kids. No way in hell is this turkey a general.

"Hey there, cherry."

Everyone seated leans to get a look at the new voice at the party. King shitbird squints up at me, annoyed, but not yet sure how much heat he should put behind that look. You run into all types in Bangkok.

"What did you call me?" he says.

"You the FNG, right?" I say with a chummy laugh. "I mean, around here. You definitely the FNG."

"The fuck does that mean?"

I smile. It means I'm right, and it means that it's on.

"You gonna ask me to sit down, cherry? We brothers, right? Yeah, we brothers. Come on, gimme them DAPs."

"I don't know who you think you're talking to, friend, but you best keep right on steppin.'"

I squat down with my sore spider legs, speak softly into his ear. "I ain't your friend, and I ain't steppin' for nobody."

He pulls away and turns, finding my eyes. All of my eyes. What he sees there pushes the shiny skin back on his face. He hides it with a smile, closing the furnace doors. He raises his hand, offered up to the growling dog. You let it get your scent, and it maybe won't rip out your throat, right? "Pull up a seat, son," he says.

"Oh, you my daddy now?"

He laughs. "Oh, I ain't your daddy, *boy*," he says, emphasizing the "boy" like guys like him always did. I dealt with that shit for years up north, until I dropped the bayou just long enough to get the fuck out of there for good, trading insults in English for taunts across the wire in Vietnamese. "But I do have manners."

"Nah, you don't. You're a swine, rolling in the mud and showing your ass."

"You looking for trouble?"

"Wasn't. But I think I found some."

"War's over, soldier."

"No, it isn't. Not for any of us who were there. It'll never be over. But you wouldn't know that, would you? You're an actor. A clown in a costume." I'm getting heated. His group is getting nervous.

"Let me buy you a drink," he said, holding up a finger.

"Let me buy *you* one," I say, slapping down a few bills. "At the hotel up the street. This place ain't for you."

He's backed into a corner. Fight or flight, and the latter would kill the party and his rep, whatever that may be with whomever these people are. The former? Well, we'd just have to see. "Why don't you mind your own fucking business?" he says.

"Because what you're talking about, in this place, *is* my business. We're guests here. Act accordingly."

"You're an uppity one, ain't you?"

I lean in close, smelling his sweat and everything he ate and drank for the last hour. "I'm as uppity as they come."

He sizes me up, looking for angles. Bloodshot eyes narrow. "You ain't military."

"Not currently. Not anymore."

---

*T. E. GRAU*

"Probably went AWOL," he says with a snort, bringing his drink to his mouth like a canteen. "No steel in the spine."

Now my blood's up, bubbling atop of that heat. I'd pull some Military Occupation Specialties and see where it takes us. Shit, I already know where it'd take us, and I can't wait for us to arrive.

"What company were you in?" I ask.

"Special Forces."

"Like hell. What station?"

"You think I'm going to tell you?"

"What's your MOS?"

"I ain't telling you that, neither."

He's not even good at the lie. Too lazy. Clown in a costume.

"Where'd you do basic?" I continue.

"Nothing basic about anything I did," he says with a self-satisfied sniff, taking a drink.

"I'd say everything about you is basic."

Somehow, that gets to him. Touches too close to trailer-park siding. Dogshit in a dirt backyard. "Maybe I'll start asking you questions," he says, face flushing a deeper shade of rose. "How'd you like that, smart ass?"

"No, just one more from me, then the floor is yours."

"Shoot," he says, leaning back and throwing out his crotch.

"What does the inside of a man look like?"

This takes him by surprise, slides his groin back into the folds of his chair. He stumbles backward through the booze-soaked chemicals of his brain, looking for any movie, book, or science text to come up with the proper answer, to shut this crazy motherfucker down.

"Red," he says finally in a low voice. He hopes it has the effect of past pain, but I know it's the whimper of defeat.

"No," I say, shaking my head. "It's black."

Less than two minutes later, the table is empty, his beret left on the table.

I regard that hat, sitting among the empty glasses. Dead soldiers, the civs call them. We wouldn't dare. Maybe I'll trade this hat for mine back in the cave. Maybe I'll move what's inside that bush hat into this new cover, if it'll fit. If it'll stay. Maybe I'll just keep drinking right here and never go back to the cave again, because something in there is eventually going to eat me.

There's something behind me now, watching me. Maybe I never left the cave, and I'm still sitting in that chair. Maybe it followed me here, but it never has before.

No, what's behind me isn't a *thing*, my new eyes tell me. It's just a man. Which means I am where I think I am, I did drive a table full of playtime assholes into the street, and I am sitting at that same table with a man watching me. I've had enough of men tonight. Let me watch, then move the fuck one. Petting zoo is close.

"Handy work with our friend," the man says, his voice bemused. He was closer than I thought.

"He ain't my friend." I look at the man standing just behind me to the right, note his pale skin, the dark circles under his black eyes that seem like they're all pupil, so dilated they eat up the light. I've seen him before, and he's obviously seen me. Somehow I knew he'd talk to me some day, and I'd just given him the perfect in. "He *isn't* my friend, either."

"May I?"

I shrug. I honestly don't care, and now I have to catch up on my buzz before the money runs out.

He sits and smiles at me, almost with pride. "American, just like I thought."

"What else would I be?"

"African. Yemeni. Hell, you could have been Haitian."

"Maybe I'm all those. Haitian-born African who grew up in Yemen."

"No, you're not. You're an American through and through. Hard to place your accent, though."

I don't know how to take this, nor do I know how to take him. He's coming on like he knows me, and that he might is what scares me. I don't want anyone to know me anymore, especially not here, and especially not someone on Uncle Sam's payroll, which this dude obviously is.

"I've seen you around," he says.

"I kind of stick out." I motion to the bartender for another drink.

"What brings you to Bangkok?"

"I was born here."

"Reborn, maybe," he says with a plastic grin, proud of himself. He's probably proud of himself a lot.

"Nah, I was reborn out in the jungle."

"Vietnam?"

"Sure wasn't the Congo."

"So what brings you to Bangkok?"

"Are we going to have a problem?" I shoot him a look, almost daring him to answer the question a certain way. I'm still pissed from the jive-ass turkey in the hat.

"I certainly hope not," he says, not the least bit worried. "That's not why I sat down."

"Then why did you? Reminisce about the red, white, and blue? Talk some Yankees? Cleveland Browns?"

"No, no. I don't need that. Not from you, certainly."

The drink arrives. The bartender looks at the man, who pays for my drink and ignores the offer of change.

"I don't trust nobody who doesn't drink," I say.

"I don't trust anyone, period."

"Smart move."

"The only move."

I gulp my drink, faster than normal, because I want to get out of here, away from this self-satisfied cadaver and his weird eyes who keeps looking at me like he knows me, or has a secret. Maybe some combination of both.

"I'm going to ask you for a favor," the man says. "You don't have to do it, but I'm going to ask anyway, because that's what I do, and I've been wanting to for a while. Is that okay?"

"No harm in asking, I guess."

"That's not always the case, but I hope in this one it is."

I finish my drink and push the glass to the center of the table, joining the rest of the empties. Only one dead solider here.

"I know who you work for," he says.

"No you don't."

"Yeah. Yeah I do."

I look him in the eyes. "No, you really don't, and it would be better for you if you didn't, you dig?"

"Okay, let's do it that way if you'd like."

I get up, looking around to see who is watching me. Everyone is and isn't. Same old. Blind eyes watching you everywhere, shadows in every corner, waiting inside spider webs. "I gotta go."

"But I haven't asked my favor yet."

"I don't do favors."

"Maybe for me you will. I'm a very appreciative person, with lots of friends. Doing a favor for someone like me could be quite beneficial to a stranger in a strange land without many friends of his own."

"I don't need friends."

"Everyone needs friends, Mr. Broussard."

I drop back into my seat. "How do you know my name?" I know how he does, but in the moment, I can't help but ask.

"How does anyone know anything?" The reflections of the bar lights in his flat black eyes flash like midnight quartz. He's now deep in his game, and loving every move of it.

I stare at him, noting his smile, his stiff posture, the way his hands don't move as they rest palm down on the table. He could be a ventriloquist dummy. Might be. The bartender is watching me, and I signal for another drink. However this goes, I know I'm going to need it.

"My favor is simple," he continues. "Tiny, in fact. All I'm asking is that during your normal workday, if you happen to run across some interesting information that can't be traced back to you, that can help me out just a bit, get something on the books, justify my existence in this strange little town, then I'd surely appreciate it, and be obliged to return a favor to you."

"You CIA? Military Intelligence? One of those Nixon drug hounds?"

The man's face betrays nothing. Just that same, unwavering smile. The rest of his body doesn't move a muscle.

"Yeah, okay. I heard through the grapevine that the military is backing certain ex-generals and current warlords in the drug game, positioning rooks and knights based on who's down with the communists and who still digs Uncle Sam."

"This grapevine of yours sounds a tad unreliable."

"This grapevine is making all the wine that brings out all the drunks, and you know that. That's why you sat down, and that's why you're in this 'strange little town.'"

The man studies me as my new drink arrives. He doesn't pay for it this time. I reach into my pocket and toss whatever I can find in it on the table. The man notices it's the last bit of cash I have. Shouldn't have reached into my pocket.

"Do you like living here, Mr. Broussard?"

"I don't like living anywhere."

"Then why don't you just...stop?"

I look up into the corners of the room, out of habit. Survival. "It's complicated."

"Yes, it usually is," he says.

"You seem to like living here just fine," I say.

"No, I really don't. I know guys that would, which is why they sent me here. Knew I'd stay focused on the task at hand." He looks around the room, out into the teeming street, still buzzing with neon and small groups of holiday carousers this late into the morning, hoping to push back the dawn. "I'd much rather be in my garden with my wife, drinking coffee and giving the world the finger through the vines growing up the high privacy walls."

"Could have fooled me."

"Yeah, well, that's my job, isn't it?"

"I guess."

"You guessed right." He gets to his feet, the puppet finding his legs. He slides his hands into his pockets. "Think about that favor, and come find me if you want to position me as a man beholden. Me being obliged to someone usually works out pretty well for them." He tosses down some bills. "In case you're thirsty."

"I ain't."

"Everyone's thirsty."

He walks away from the table, out the front door, and out into the street, disappearing immediately into the formless movements of a nighttime crowd.

I look at the cash on the table, then think about the cave, what happened right before I left.

The drink is down my throat and the glass climbs into the air.

## Chapter Seventeen

## Punji Sticks

That was too much money.

I drank too goddamn much.

That was too much money.

Can't feel my feet.

Street is sideways tonight.

Them dudes up ahead. They don't look right.

Not them dudes. Those dudes. Keep your head, motherfucker.

Those dudes.

These dudes.

Now they're behind. They look even worse now.

Must think I have money.

Ain't that a bitch?


I can't feel it, but I can hear it, like I'm remembering it.

If I pass out, I hope I die.

If I go into a coma, Black Shuck will have its way with me.

If I die, it'll do worse. It'll take me in with it.

If I pass out, it'll have me.

If I die, before I wake.

I pray the Lord.

My eyes to take.
Gunshots.
No, not gunshots.
Sticks shooting through skin.
Pop. Pop. Pop.
Punctured meat.
Blood on me.
Can't feel the bullets.
No, not bullets.
Sticks.
Punji sticks.
Can't feel the fists.
They think I have money.
Ain't that a bitch?

More gunshots.
No, not bullets.
Sticks.
Punji sticks.
More blood.
More and more and more blood.

The blood is a River.
Taking me back to the jungle.
I'm getting close.
To the cave of bones.
Where I can find rest.

Can't feel a thing.

## Chapter Eighteen

## Chapter Eighteen

## Night Vision

Broussard watched Chapel, like he often had since the first moment he'd met him. There was something about the set of the man's jaw, and the calm, almost bemused gleam of those boyish eyes positioned just right amongst the wrinkles that was comforting to Broussard, and he assumed, the rest of the men, if they took time to notice it or not. Certain people were made to be leaders, or took to it naturally when command was foisted upon them by circumstance. Broussard's grandmother was like that, serving as the anchor of the neighborhood, an organizer, a *presence*. "Mama Broussard," they'd call her, even those kids who had their own mamas. Even mamas themselves. Chapel was one of these people. A soothing presence. A rock in the middle of a rushing stream, cutting through the scattering force and remaining steadfast and hard, always there to hold your arm as you stepped across the water.

Chapel's eyes squinted into the night that leaked into their open door, combing through the impossibly black nothingness with such intensity that Broussard was convinced the man could pull whatever he was looking for, no matter how far away, how hidden, out of the nothingness and into the low light, allowing him to see it for what it was. To find what he was looking for against all odds of probability and physics. Broussard watched Chapel watch the outside. He wanted to see what this man saw, or at least witness the moment when he finally accomplished his goal. And Broussard knew that he would, as men like that didn't do things for no reason, just for show. He was hunting, Chapel was, cutting the night with those keen gray eyes that sliced through the nonsense to find the bloody heart of the matter. The drone of the machinery inside the shell of metal above their heads wrapped them all in a familiar bubble that was difficult to push through, and none wanted to except for Chapel, who trained his eyes outside, hunting.

"Here," Chapel said, barely audible inside the pocket of sound. But Broussard heard it, without seeing his lips move. "Here!" Chapel shouted, and pointed out into the black.

All eyes followed the gesture. Broussard leaned toward the open door, to get a better view. He saw nothing, only black.

"We've found the last front line, gentlemen," Chapel yelled out above the drone. "The war ends right here!"

## Chapter Nineteen

## Angels with Dirty Faces

I wake up, and for the first time that I can remember, nothing is sitting on my chest but a stabbing pain, and it feels like freedom.

No hound. No witch. My bed isn't on fire, or sinking into the swamp. No bag on my head, no barrel in my mouth. No River, below me or inside. All I can feel is pain, and all I can see is the girl's face. The girl from outside the cave, who came calling for the Night Man.

"You live?"

I move my mouth, but no sound comes out. The girl gives me a drink of water from a cracked ceramic bowl. The bowl is light blue. The coolness of the water brings my voice back.

"Where is it?" I say. My lips are cut, swollen.

The girl seems confused at first, but then nods slightly. "She no." She thinks about what she said, then tries again, motioning to the floor. "She no...*let* here." The girl points at the old woman, who is seated in the corner. Her eyes are closed and she is mumbling something. Whatever she's saying, I know that it kept Black Shuck away. For now.

I try to sit up, but I can't. Everything hurts. Very little moves.

"No," the girl says.

"What happened?" I ask.

She makes a fist and buries it into her other hand, then forms her finger into a pistol. "*Bung, bung,*" she says, jerking back her hand like the kick of a gun. She touches the bulging knot over my left eye, the gash on my cheek, then the bandage around my left shoulder and chest muscle. I realize that's where the pain is coming from.

I peel back the bandage. A foul-smelling poultice has been packed into a long, hot gash. Just a flesh wound. The bullet grazed me, never went inside. Maybe the only bit of luck I've ever had.

Exhaling and clearing the white stars clouding my vision, I look around the tiny, rectangular room. Partially caved-in ceiling ringed with mold stains shaped like howling mouths. Brass chimes hang in the corners, tinkling to each other. Cracked plaster walls, covered over by prayer sheets written in large Chinese symbols. The framed picture of a young man in a North Vietnamese officer's uniform, looking off to the right, eyes full of edge and determination. The cement floor is clean but stained with the eternal damp of every ground level in the Floating City. An opium pipe rests on a wooden block next to me, the bowl blackened from recent use. Must have been part of the medical treatment. They probably burnt through a pound to put me down, not counting on my level of dedicated tolerance.

I rub my eyes. The details of the attack come back to me in sketchy, yellowed glimpses, like strobes flashing from a dirty light bulb.

"Thank you for helping me… Saving me."

She nods once, then squeezes my hand. Her grip is tight, incredibly strong.

"I hep, Night Man. You hep…we."

I groan. "I can't."

"Can, can!"

"No, I can't. I'm not the Night Man. I'm nobody like that."

"No, you all. You all. You Night Man. You hep."

"How? How can I help you? I can't even help myself. Look at me."

She puts her face very close to mine, almost touching her cheek to the tears now running down my bristly cheeks.

"You hep you, you hep us."

"What?"

"You hep you, you hep us."

I don't understand. My face tells her as much.

She points at my chest, then touches the side of my head, flutters her fingers over each of my eyes, then points to the middle of my forehead.

"You hep you, you hep us. *Vâng?*"

Yes. I know what she is saying. Somehow, I know. I nod to let her know that I do.

She nods back, exhales, then smiles. It's a beautiful thing to see.

In the corner, her grandmother starts to sing.

## Chapter Twenty

## The Plain of Jars

Before the skids touched the ground, each helicopter cut its engines, bringing their full weight of metal, men, and equipment down hard on the dried grass. In the dark, the men spilled out of their Huey and followed Chapel to the Chinook, the double set of heavy blades whooping over their heads.

They were on open tableland, dotted with boulders and trees, lit a dusky blue. Exposed country, dangerous. Broussard set down his pack, stretched his spine and gazed up at the sky. The moon was full, or nearly so, looking like a wide-open marble eye. Away from its cold white stare, a ghostly blanket of stars that made up the rest of the galaxy puffed and swirled in a dance far too massive, slow, and important for anyone to detect, captured as a snapshot a billion years old. Broussard had been looking up at the night sky for as long as he could remember, but never that he remembered had the universe seemed so close to the earth as it was out on this Laotian plain. All it would take was a determined jump from either side to cross over to the other.

"Where are we now?" McNulty said, tossing down his gear.

"We could be home."

"Stop being fucking weird, Broussard. Can you do me that favor?"

The bay door to the Chinook dropped open, exposing a huge, carefully arranged stack of crates and unlabeled boxes, lashed tight with nylon cording.

"Who's gonna hump all this shit?" McNulty said.

"Chapel says help's coming," Render said.

"Guardian angels with a fucking moving van?"

Broussard climbed the ramp, unhooked the stabilizing cords and started unloading, handing off the first box to Chapel, who grinned.

"Can you feel it, Broussard?"

"Feel what, sir?"

"The end."

Nearly an hour later, the men leaned against the stacks they'd assembled on the grass, tired and sweating, as the three helicopters fired up and darted into the brightening sky at a tight angle, staying low as they gained speed and headed back toward the southeast, in the direction of Vietnam, the sound of their blades slapping at the exposed granite mountain peaks and sandstone bluffs that surrounded this elevated upland.

McNulty looked around as the emerging sun brought slow illumination to the landscape. "Where are we, sir?"

"Don't matter where we are, numbnuts," Darby said, loading his rifle.

"It might not to you, trailer rat, but it does to me."

"Just do your goddamn job," Darby said, lighting a cigarette.

"This is the Xieng Khouang Plateau," Chapel said from the edge of the hill overlooking the lower hill country. "West of Phonsavan."

"Yeah, that's exactly what I thought," McNulty said dryly.

"Don't ask questions you don't want answers to, McNulty," Morganfield said as he passed by to join Chapel at the edge of the hill overlooking the valley, murmuring softly into the radio.

"The mute finally speaks, and it's to bust my balls. How do you like that?"

"I like it just fine," Render said.

"This don't look like no jungle," Darby said, slinging his M-14 over his shoulder. "Better sight lines." He smiled at Broussard. "I like it." Darby walked away from the group, whistling.

"Man, don't jinx this shit," Render said. "I'll walk my black ass all over God's green, long as there ain't no jungle involved."

"You'd think you'd be used to it by now," McNulty said, sprouting a grin when Render looked at him.

"Chuck, I'm not gonna take that shit the way I think you meant it. For *your* sake, you dig?"

"I will," Broussard said, surprising McNulty, and everyone else in the group.

"Chicago's an idiot," Medrano said. "Don't listen to a word he says."

"The name's McNulty, Medrrrano," McNulty said, trying to roll the r without success.

"Haven't yet," Render said. "Won't start now."

The thud of bombs in the distance silenced everyone, bringing them back to the reality of the wider world.

McNulty peered up into the sky. "I didn't hear no jets."

"B-52s," Broussard said. "High altitude."

"What're Big Uglies doing in Laos?"

"The same thing we're doing here," Render said, his face grim. "Nothing, right? Not a goddamn thing."

Chapel and Morganfield rejoined the group, putting away maps and holstering their radios.

"You think anyone saw us land, sir?" McNulty said.

"No, I do not," Chapel said.

"We're pretty exposed out here, though," Broussard said.

"Yes, we are."

"Permission to speak openly, sir?" McNulty said.

"Do you ever speak any other way?"

McNulty paused. "Permission to speak, sir."

"You don't need to ask me for permission. This isn't grade school."

"I think we're open to attack here, sir. Mortar fire, at the very least."

Medrano snorted. "General McNulty."

"No one's firing on us here," Chapel said, making a count of the stacked crates.

"No enemy in the area?" Broussard said.

"Not at present, no. I called ahead to make sure the area was cleared first. But even if there are a few stray Victor Charlie who wander close, they won't attack us here."

"Why would you say that?" McNulty said.

"Because it's the truth," Morganfield said. No one liked McNulty, even the guy who was barely there.

"Yeah, but why's it the truth?"

"Darby is about to tell you," Chapel said, clamping the pipe between his back teeth.

"Y'all need to check this out," Darby called from the edge of the plateau, where we was glassing the hill country below with a pair of binoculars.

The rest of the men jogged over to Darby and looked out onto the topography below.

Grassland stretched out for miles, dotted with trees, boulders, and smaller grayish objects all nearly the same size, grouped together in clusters that stretched across the entire expanse.

"Check out them rocks," Darby said, handing the binoculars to Broussard, who put them to his eyes. "They don't seem to be random."

The smaller gray objects were oblong, hollowed out like urns, a yard or two high, worn rough by weather and mottled by lichens. Hundreds of them, maybe thousands, as it was difficult to tell them apart from the large stones scattered between them.

"Gravestones?" Broussard said, more to himself.

---

T. E.  GRAU

"Something like that," Chapel said.

"What kind of place is this?" Medrano said, performing the sign of the cross across his chest.

"The Plain of Jars," Chapel said.

The men stared down at the ancient stone structures scattered out for a mile in front of them. Patterns emerged briefly, but were easily scattered. Whatever had survived the grind of history only offered hints now, not secrets revealed.

"We walking through that?" McNulty said.

"Right through," Chapel said.

"Can't we walk around it?"

"No, we cannot."

"Don't seem right."

"You superstitious, McNulty?" Darby said.

"I never used to be," McNulty said. "These days, though? Man… If ghost are real, they live out here."

Chapel started to laugh. Morganfield hid a smile. The other men looked at each other, confused.

Movement came from behind them. Broussard turned to find fifty Hmong men, dressed identically in American-style fatigues, standing in a semi-circle around the mound of gear. No one had heard them approach.

Chapel's laughter settled into a smile. He walked to the Hmong and greeted them warmly in their native tongue, shaking hands and gripping shoulders. The mayor of every square inch he walked.

Render slapped the back of McNulty's helmet, knocking it askew. "There's your fucking moving van."

Half of the Hmong soldiers lashed a crate or duffle or roll of cable to their backs, trudged down the plateau, and set off across the Plain of Jars without a word. The remaining two dozen Hmong marched noisily in the opposite direction, talking and singing as they headed toward the wall of trees to the southeast.

"Where're they going?" Broussard asked Chapel as the officer passed by, walking in the direction of the equipment.

"They're making a path," Chapel said. "Our route from this drop, at least in the eyes on the VC. They'll be sure to be extra noisy and obvious with the trail they cut, performing in the manner of the United States military and not like a local."

"So where are *they* going?" Broussard indicated the Hmong carrying the equipment, now well onto the plain below.

Chapel smiled. "Our way." He laid a hand on Broussard's shoulder, then turned to the men. "Mount up and follow. Eyes open and powder ready." Chapel walked away, joining Morganfield working the radio, and headed out in the direction of the gear.

The men fell in behind them, adjusting their straps, checking their chambers, and finding their pace.

"This is the only way to hump," Medrano said with a grin.

"If you think that, how all them babies of yours born?" Render said.

Medrano grinned, too blissed out by the lightness of his load to talk any shit in return.

"Don't sit right with me," Darby said, pinching out his cigarette and stashing the butt inside his vest. "We can all carry our own weight. *Should* all."

"Run up there and volunteer then," McNulty said. "No one's stopping you."

Darby frowned. "This division of labor into race and class is bullshit. Straight up."

"Ol' Chairman Mao, right here in our unit," McNulty said. "Can you beat that?"

"I ain't chairman of nothin', and Mao can kiss my pearly white country ass. But right is right."

"Man, if Darby weren't such a peckerwood, I'd swear he's a brother," Render said.

"We all brothers on the inside," Darby said. "All the way back to Africa."

"Say that shit when the gookers come for you," McNulty said.

"I have, and I will," Darby said.

"Ain't that about something?" Render said with a laugh. "White man talking about some Africa."

"Redneck hippie," McNulty said, shaking his head and spitting. "If that don't beat all."

"Listen, y'all," Darby said, "I'm gonna be real clear, okay? I've been hired by my country, by my *employer*, to kill, and I *will* kill. Continually, and with great effectiveness. But unlike some of these rock-kickin' bozos out here—" he looked at McNulty—"I have respect for my enemy, as my enemy is my brother who just happened to be born on the opposite team, which makes him blameless in intent. Different uniforms, is all. Playin' the same sport, all wantin' to win the same game."

"See what I mean, Crayfish?" Render said, nudging Broussard. "Dude's straight up Negro."

"Yeah, he's something else," Broussard said, mystified.

"Will wonders never cease, Lord Jesus?" Render said, laughing.

Darby smiled, lit up a cigarette. "I just see shit, man. I just see it how it is. Y'all could, too, if you'd just get out of your own goddamn way."

McNulty picked up his pace, lashing out with his machete at branches that weren't in the way, muttering to himself. "Whole world's gone batshit."

They'd walked for over an hour through the Plain of Jars, no one saying a word as they moved through the stone ossuaries. Some were still upright, but others had shifted in the eternally damp clay, veering sideways. Several were lying on their sides, and a few had been mostly swallowed up by the earth.

Broussard stopped to inspect one of them, running his hands over the rough fungi growing on the outside in one symbiotic community of feeding and breeding fibers. He looked inside, and found a pool of brackish water, twigs and bones protruding from black surface.

"Keep away from there, Broussard."

Broussard turned his head and found Chapel watching him. "We don't want to stir up what we don't have to."

Broussard fell back into the line of walking men, thinking about how Chapel's admonition hit his ears in an odd way.

The number of stone jars thinned, then disappeared completely as the turf became thicker, taller, trading common brome for elephant grass that grew as high as a basketball rim. Up ahead, a hundred-foot-high barrier of jungle waited.

Broussard turned around to take a last look at the jars, but they were above him now, bones in water, sitting out another eon.

## Chapter Twenty-One

## Come Tell Me Your Ghosts

We walk together, the girl and me, through a warren of cramped alleyways under dark clouds clotting the sky. Just minutes ago, we were on a paved street bordering the Chao Phraya River, with its familiar sounds of the port, smell of sewage and rotting fish, and the buzz of scooter traffic. Now, a dozen steps and two turns off the street, I find myself instantly lost on a muddy track inside a part of the Floating City that I've never seen before, as I wasn't granted access to take it in. But today I've been shown the way in, and creep through the filthy brown arteries of a beast I don't fully understand.

The alleys are narrow, littered with spat-out refuse of forgotten people, places, and things. Those discarded nouns. Weed trees and creepers split through crumbling cement-brick walls painted blue. A decaying train track bisects the block and disappears into a stack of ingeniously designed shacks and open-wall junk markets. The ground is slick but worn smooth, a mixture of old cobblestones and brick, recent cement, and pools of briny water seeping up from below. Trash is everywhere, fusing with the ground, the walls, filling in the cracks like mortar.

We pass a skeletal man squatting on a piece of cardboard, looking out into nothing through a pair of large spectacles. A dog sits patiently next to him, staring at his face, as if waiting for instruction. Children huddle together over a hole in the brick, looking down into it and pointing, talking quietly in awed tones. I wonder what could be down there. I feel as if they know, and are waiting anxiously to show the rest of us what lives in the hollow earth. There is no wind here, but the sound of crushed humanity is everywhere, lingering on the dead air.

The girl is holding my hand. I haven't held anyone's hand for longer than I can remember. Not like this, anyway. Her fingers are slender, grip strong, her skin warm and pale against my own. It's that feminine hand that has so much more power in this world than one rough and hard. Soft hands build. Hard ones destroy. I feel as if I'm falling in love with her, this girl, but that doesn't make sense. Not in the normal way I know. She's a baby. She's my baby, just starting to get grown, and we're walking together to Sunday school for a few steps. We round a corner and I'm taking her to the winter dance. She pulls on my hand, leading me down a narrow passageway between crumbling buildings, and then I imagine for a moment that I'm walking her to school on her first day. I look at her and smile. A hard-faced woman hisses at us from an empty window, and the feeling slips away. The girl is a stranger leading me to what could be my doom, and I'm letting her, because I've been heading there for years on my own, and I appreciate the company. I don't know her name, because I don't need to. She doesn't know mine, because I don't have one that fits anymore. I'm the Night Man, and that's good enough for her.

She stops and looks up, not letting go of my hand. I follow her eyes. In front of us is a massive old French colonial mansion, jammed between a collapsed cement building and a rectangular tower of scaffolding covered in corrugated tin roof panels wired together like a patchwork of poorly sewn sections of rusted skin. The dichotomy of the scene makes it seem as if a giant child hid away an elaborate doll house amid the ruins of a bombed village.

The house is mesmerizing, weather-worn but still lushly ornate and somehow profane with its cornices and baroque touches in such a mean place. Angels and demons taunt each other at the peaks of gambrel roofs topping mini balconies and stairways that wind behind the walls, leading to secret places or possibly nowhere at all. Every window still holds its thick leaded glass, crisscrossed by corroded brass framing, splitting the human faces that look out from them, watching the two of us down below. Generations of damp and the unstable underbelly of the Floating City have shifted the structure several degrees, its stone foundation sticking up above the street, giving the impression that it had been knocked in the head and stayed that way. The tilted porch is lined with people, mostly old women, who look down on us with no expression.

The girl points to the top floor, where a single window has been shuttered, held tight by a knotted chain of copper given over to a tarnish of green. Her face is grave. "Nói với họ những bóng ma của bạn," she says.

"I don't understand," I say.

The rain begins to fall, the sky unable to hold back any longer, and bathes everything below it. A chewed-up river of water pours down in increments from the universe miles above the clouds.

The front door, set deep in the porch, opens, but no one emerges. It's an invitation, and we take it.

## Chapter Twenty-Two

## Dead Between the Walls

We escape the rain through the open door, and drip onto a threadbare rug that was clearly once a thick, glorious piece of work worn down by years and the comings and goings of a million pair of feet.

Benches are set up in the spacious foyer, where dozens of people sit quietly, even the babies not making a peep. A wide staircase bisects the back of the structure, leading up in a gently segmented spiral to the floors above. There's a hush to the entire house, except for the rain outside and the sounds coming from the upper levels. Thumps, groans, guttural words and growls. Someone screams for what seems like a minute straight. I can't tell if it's a man or a woman, so stripped down and raw are the tones of it. Chimes tinkle above the door without the aid of wind.

I find myself looking at the ceiling like everyone else in the room when a woman enters from a side passageway. She stands in the exact center of the foyer, her greenish eyes expressionless.

"I am Clotilde," she says, her enunciated English clinging to the vestiges of a French accent. Her face is lined and handsome, chestnut hair shot with silver, and her attire looks as if Victorian finery slowly went native, adding in colored silks and flowers to the dour black of formal dress. I could imagine that she was born with the house, and arrived with it from wherever it came from, weathering the elements and adapting with the creep of age.

She waits for us to say something, hands clasped in front of her, but I have no idea what to say, nor why I'm here. The girl continues staring at the ceiling, listening to the disturbing noises and moving her mouth in silent prayer.

"Is this your place?" I ask.

"Mine? No, *monsieur*, it is yours." She points at the girl. "And it is hers." She looks at the faces from the porch through the window inside. "It is theirs." She folds her hands in front of her and regards us evenly.

The girl puts her hand on my chest. "*Anh ta có một con ma,*" she says.

The woman nods.

"What is she saying?" I ask.

"She says you have a ghost."

The girl nods. "*Con ma đang cố giết nó.*"

I look at Clotilde.

"She says it is trying to kill you."

My mouth goes dry. "Yes."

"*Tôi nghĩ anh ấy đã chết.*"

Clotilde walks up to me and looks into my face. She pokes my cheek with her finger, pinching the skin. She pries open each of my eyes, then my mouth, and looks down my throat, sniffing the air leaking out.

"What are you doing?" I say, pulling away. I don't want anyone touching me. Not like that.

"She thinks you might be dead already."

I try to say something, but pause. "Am I?" The question sounds stupid, but I'm genuinely curious.

"We shall see."

She takes us up the staircase, which seems to ascend four or five floors. Maybe more. It's hard to tell, as the darkness clouding the uppermost ceiling takes in the staircase without showing there it ends. Standing outside, I could have sworn this was a three-story affair, but the house seems to climb forever. At each landing, there are several shrines set up in corners, shallow alcoves. Most of them appear to be Buddhist. Some of them are in supplication to something else, sporting animal bones arranged in crowns, skins stuffed with dried herbs and flowers long dead. Thorns piercing through shriveled bits of mummified flesh. Death magic. Ghost worship. The sounds from the upper rooms have gone quiet.

After climbing an unknown number of floors, we step off onto a long hallway. Much like the height of this house, the width and length confuse the brain, as it seem far too wide or long or deep for the outside visual constraints. Closed doors line the corridor. There are so many closed doors, with one at the far, far end of this passageway open and waiting for us. A tiny woman stands in the doorway, her small eyes reaching out and finding mine, somehow digging in behind them and slowly burrowing down.

The hum starts at the base of my skull and works its way forward, grabbing for my eyes from the back. The River is near again, winding its way toward me from wherever it comes from. Right now it's below, at the bottom of the hole in the cement surrounded by children. The River is underneath this entire city, making it float. It wants to open up the floor—all the floors—and take me from here.

Does Black Shuck control the River? Does it use it? Is it part of the River, or does it flow from it, like a stream of blood, flaming like the River burning straight through the two mountain peaks and down into the Laotian jungle?

Floor planks begin to soften, and I'm sinking. Falling back into the current, wondering where it will take me this time. Back in the jungle. No matter where I started, I'd always end up back in the jungle.

I reach out for the girl before being swept away, and a firm hand finds mine. It belongs to Clotilde, and she leads me up from the swamp in the hallway, away from the buzz and noise of the River, and into the room with the open door. The girl is beside me. My feet find firm floor as soon as I cross the threshold.

"Welcome back to dry land," Clotilde says.

I sob for some reason. Maybe relief. Maybe resignation. There's so little difference between the two these days, even on a day where a human hand doesn't let the water take me. I now realize that sob was shock.

"I almost..." I begin, not sure how to finish, dazed. "I was almost gone."

"I know," Clotilde says. "We will not let you get away this time."

I look around the room, noting the low table on the rug, the pillows, the pastoral artwork on the walls. In a corner, four musicians are prepping what appear to be instruments. I don't recognize any of them except for the flute. The tiny woman is gone.

"Before we begin, I will need whatever money you have," Clotilde says.

"I don't have..." I don't know what I have on me at this point.

"You do not need much. But we will need certain...*des offres.*"

I reach into my pocket and dig around for bill, coins, anything.

"I will need your shirt also."

I look at her, suspicious.

"And boots."

I'm starting to not like this, exposing myself in this way. "Why?"

She holds out her hand. "*S'il vous plaît?*"

I place whatever baht I have in my pocket into her palm. She hands the money to the girl, says a few words in Vietnamese, and the girl quickly leaves the room.

I look around, and see that everyone is watching me. I shouldn't be surprised, or suspicious. I'd watch me, too. I begin to unbutton my shirt. "Where's the...person that's going to do this?"

"She is coming," Clotilde says. "She is preparing."

I remove my shirt and hand it to her.

"You need to prepare, as well."

## Chapter Twenty-Three

## The Furious One

My palms have been pressed together for so long that my arms shake. Could be sore muscles, the wound in my side, or the dope sickness, as I've been away from the cave for what seems like weeks. Lazy tendrils of sweet incense smoke weave through the space between my hands and face, making shapes of things I almost recognize, before dancing away into nothingness.

I'm seated in front of a table where offerings have been laid out, all my pockets could afford, which wasn't much. A bowl of noodles, a glass of whiskey. A small paper pig rests next to an empty Coke can, surrounded by flowers. A cheap bracelet laden with such an array of rhinestones that it could only be priceless or worthless, depending on who owned it. The four musicians sit cross-legged in the corner, waiting to begin.

The medium finally entered the room after an hour wait, which was about an hour ago. Her age was hard to determine, as she was wearing stage makeup, alabaster base with red and black accents, creating the effect of a mask. Her body was covered in a long, flowing robe of brightly colored silks. She sat in front of me, her palms out, holding thin candles between each finger. Her eyes rested on me, her painted lips a tight red line. I didn't need to be a psychic to know that she didn't want me here.

"We will be in contact with the Mother Goddesses of the three realms," Clotilde said before we began, pointing to the three framed pictures on the wall depicting a divine female figure in each scene of forest, water, and heaven. "They *do not* like to be interrupted." Her tone told me everything I needed to know without asking. She then retreated to a corner of the room at my left, where I couldn't see her from my position on the floor in front of the table, dressed in my trousers and undershirt, feet bare.

Now, after this long wait, the musicians begin to play a simple, beautiful folk melody. The medium's expressionless face changes, lighting up with a smile. Eyes wide, she rises gently to her feet and performs a series of small, precise dance steps. She speaks in three different voices, her face animated, taking on characters, the mask changing with each, forming her into an entirely different person, as she implores the Mother Goddesses to grant her access to the spirit realm. She repeats this several times, as the music changes tempo and pitch. She laughs, asking again, this time trying a new character, and holds up my shirt and one of my boots. I can't imagine that any of this is going to work.

As I contemplate getting up and getting out of this place, getting back to the cave to fend for myself in a way that makes sense to me, the boot falls from the medium's hand and the cheery voice catches in her throat, staggering her. A hiss escapes her mouth as all of the air is pressed out of her lungs. The musicians continue playing, exchanging quick glances with wide eyes. I look for Clotilde but can't find her. I look for the girl, and locate her across the room, the mask of dread on her face fading from view as the candles dip and gutter in their liquid wax, swallowing the light and sending more smoke into the room. Black smoke.

The medium's sudden scream cuts the smoky air, chopping off the music, and she falls to the floor, writhing as she hits the soft rug, the many layers and colors of her robe billowing around her like the release of ink from a rainbow octopus. Her lips pull back over clenched teeth, a buzzing growl building deep in her throat.

The medium rises from her shed silk, naked and twisting at the waist like a broken music-box ballerina. Her ribs and sternum swell and pulsate, as if not connected to her spine. Things crack inside her small body, then pop, as joints detach from their sockets.

She then slowly attempts to straighten, rising up with her body slightly out of order, everything crooked and misaligned. Sweat, tears, and sticky saliva carve rivulets through her makeup, streaking her face, dripping red, white, and black down the front of her pale body.

The musicians scramble out of the room, mouthing oaths of protection. The door slams shut behind them.

I get to my feet and find Clotilde in the gloom. She has moved somehow, and is on the opposite side of me than when we began, and much further away than the room should allow.

"What's happening?" I whisper.

She shakes her head, stunned. "*Je ne sais pas.*"

The medium's mouth begins to move, but only harsh whispers slither out. Her eyes roll back in her head, and seem to come back around as solid black orbs, too large for her sockets, like those of a fly. Behind her, something large and dark, blacker than the shadows cast by the struggling candles, rises up to the ceiling. The medium flings her arms out straight from her sides. The black presence issues a thrumming vibration of sound, like a roar underwater, the low register splitting the atoms in the air and the brains of everyone in the room, bringing a chill to the air. This thing is huge and shapeless and composed of rage. I don't know if it's Black Shuck, as it doesn't look like a hound, but it also looks like nothing I've ever seen. It roars again, that weird, horrible sound, and is pushed back into the corner of the room by the medium, who stands upright, her entire body so rigid I can hear tendons creak, muscles knot and rip. She is standing on her tiptoes, but doesn't sway, as if held up by a wire looped through the top of her head.

She screams, laughs, shouts out words in garbled Vietnamese, then other languages that sound unfamiliar, vaguely inhuman. The black presence shoots from the corner and meets her in the middle of the room, impacting with a dull thud that reverberates through my bones. The medium stumbles, and Clotilde is at her side, lifting her, holding up her arms, as she begins to wail. It's a terrible sound, a familiar sound. I heard the same screams that night in Laos. She laughs again, a short, barking mess, then screams so forcefully it seems to tear her vocal cords, tapering off with a wet rasp. She shakes off Clotilde, and the larger woman is flung into a dresser.

I jump to my feet and go to Clotilde, maybe as much to help her as to find safety in numbers. The girl is already there with her and I can't seem to reach either of them, as the room keeps expanding in random and sudden directions, unfolding into confusing angles. Behind me, the naked woman crouches down, her voice a broken growl, collapsing with her. She snarls and coughs, expelling yellow mucus from her mouth, letting it run unchecked down her chin.

Then she goes silent. Her black eyes roll back into her head again and return entirely white as she rises to her feet, scanning the faces in the room while the mouth works, the nose sniffs. She begins to slowly spin on the very tips of her toes, nails digging into the rug, cutting through it to the hardwood below as she rotates like a nightmare ballerina.

She revolves on her tiny axis, knocking over the table and scattering the simple offerings, those white eyes searching each face, before finding me. She stops. One of her hands rises, then the other. Her fingers bend, squeeze tightly together, forming into a fist, then a shape resembling paws.

The invisible wire is cut and she breaks down into a crouch, heaving, sucking in huge gasps of air, her nose flaring. She drops onto her haunches like a dog, mouth open. Sounds leak out from deep down inside her that don't sound human, or even like an animal. She cocks her head to one side, then the other, and a long stream of words in Vietnamese pushes through— slow and low in register at first, then speeding up, rising in pitch, until it is a pure scream of sound constructed of rapidly blended words.

I lean back, as if that will protect me, but the sound pierces the center of me like a blade. This is a sharp pain, hurting the ears and the organs, not the dull mental rending of the last night with Chapel above the river valley.

Just as I reach my limit of agony, feeling a new seam of madness open up inside, the sound cuts off, and she collapses on the rug. She lands heavily and awkwardly, like a dropped deer, nothing catching her fall. Things break inside her, or maybe just return to how they should be, which might be worse.

Clotilde goes to her, pulls back her eyelids, presses two fingers to her neck.

"Is she dead?" I whisper, my head ringing, the chambers of my heart flexing to steady themselves. I feel turned inside out.

"Close."

"Will she die… because of this?"

"I-I do not know," Clotilde says, a spooked expression on her face. Something that I imagine is very unfamiliar to her, the way she wears it. "I do not know what this is."

"I hope I… If I caused…"

"What is one more?" Her look is challenging, fear twisting to loathing. She is resentful that I'm here, angry about what I've done now that she knows, and requiring the type of services that can kill one of her seers. "Wait downstairs," she says coldly, and returns to tending to the woman on the floor, covering her with the discarded robe.

I walk to the door and look back at the girl I came with, the girl who showed up at the doorway of the Night Man and saved his life, asking for a simple favor that he wouldn't grant because he's a selfish, craven motherfucker. She saved my life twice, maybe three times, and I don't know her name. I never asked, and she never offered. Because she's not like me. She's not a selfish, craven motherfucker. I am ashamed that I don't know her name and don't know her but want her to leave with me. I need someone on my side.

She doesn't look at me, her head turned away, focused on those deeper shadows in the room, where the black thing stood up. She is rocking slightly, humming a tune I don't recognize.

I leave the room, alone. I never see her again.

I wait downstairs, looking out the front door, at the mist swirling outside the house, obscuring the rest of the Floating City that waits beyond. The rain has stopped, or maybe it never rained at all. I might have spent a year in this house.

Clotilde stands at the foot of the stairs, her hands folded in front of her. I didn't hear her descend.

"What is it?" I say, not turning around but seeing her with my new set of eyes now starting to age. They're getting tired. The foyer is full of people waiting, but they seem like furniture to me, part of the house without eyes or ears. I'm back inside myself again, utterly alone in crowded room.

"It is not a dog," she says.

"I know that."

"It takes the shape of a dog."

"Why?" I say. "Why does it look like that?"

"To…scare you," Clotilde says, finding the right word in English, realizing that it doesn't do the meaning any justice.

"If it's not that, not a dog, then what is it? What is it really?"

"Un furieux," Clotilde says.

"A Furious One." I turn around. "I don't understand."

"It is one who is angry," Clotilde says. "With you."

"Why is it angry with me?"

"You know the reason."

"I don't. I don't," I say, approaching her, wanting to grab her and make her understand. I stop several feet away, never trusting my hands anymore. "I wouldn't be here if I did."

"You do, you just refuse to...admit."

"Whatever I did, let me apologize. I'll apologize..." I look up the staircase, address the ceiling and the floors above, filled with dusty, heavy air scented with mildew and incense and rotting flowers. "I'm sorry!"

"You cannot apologize. That will not work, and will not change anything. It will not..." She gestures with her hands, needing help with an abstraction. "Move the particles, no?"

"Move the particles?"

"You can only return what you have stolen," she says, refolding her hands.

"I haven't stolen anything. I don't *have* anything. You think I have anything? I don't have shit in this world."

Clotilde's face gives away nothing. "The Furious One thinks otherwise."

I collapse to the floor, holding the side of my face, feeling a little bit more of sanity slip into my fingers. "I don't understand. I don't understand any of this."

Clotilde sits on her knees and places a hand on my shoulder. "It is a Wandering Soul, this Furious One. It cries out to be buried in the ground of its ancestors."

"I don't... I don't..." But I do. I know now. But it's impossible. All of it. I hear the River roaring underneath me. It clogs my ears, blotting out her voice. The English makes no sense. She realizes this, and comes to me in French, taking me back to the bayou.

"*Avez-vous tué...les gens au Vietnam?*"

I nod my head.

"*Beaucoup?*"

I shake my head.

"*Combien?*"

I hold up one finger.

"*Avez-vous tué cet homme dans son village? Sur le terrain de sa famille?*"

I shake my head.

"*Si ses restes retournaient au village?*"

I shake my head.

"*Comment le savez-vous avec certitude?*"

I look at her. I don't have the English for this either. Sensing this, she finds hers again, if only to give me back the voice of my adult life. My childhood in the bayou can't keep me safe anymore. It never did anyway, acting only as an accomplice in bringing me here. The River drops out from under me, leaving me on the clammy rug, spongy from the rain and smelling like cats.

"Did you take a part of this man with you?"

I nod my head.

"Do you still have it?"

I nod my head.

Clotilde sits back, a look of concern tinged with disgust on her face. "Why would you do this?"

"I don't know... I don't remember..."

She looks at me for a long time, judging what she can see that's coming to the surface. "You know what you must do."

I hold my head in my hands, trying to keep it together before it explodes. Tears start to form in my eyes, and I pinch them away with my lids. "I don't know where it is anymore. I never knew."

"You must find a way." She leans in closer, taking my hand in hers. "If you are to find peace, and remove the Furious One from your scent."

*Hell hound on my trail.* The lyrics snake their way inside my head. The look on Clotilde's face shows that they also came out of my mouth.

"The spirit realm knows nothing of hell, of heaven," she says. "Only what is real, and what we think is real."

I look up at the top of the grand staircase, hoping to see the girl, her wispy frame, standing in the darkness. "I'm sorry," I say. But no one is there.

On the way back to the cave, cutting through the fog that dissipates the further I get from the house, no one calls me Night Man. No one looks at me at all. I'm not here anymore.

Underneath the Floating City, the River rushes on, leaching into the invisible jungle. Everything in life eventually ends up back in the jungle. I want it to take me there. I want the River to take me anywhere tonight, but it refuses, because it knows to leave me here, with myself and no one else in a city where I don't belong, stalked by a cosmic hound and afraid to sleep, is the worst sentence of all.

## Chapter Twenty Four

### Everything's Green Here

Operation Algernon had been five days in the jungle. Chapel had promised no more than two before they reached their objective. The men noticed.

One would think that being drowned in the green hell for days on end would warp time, mash it down into one long smudge of wet, pain, sweat, and fear. But being in the jungle made them pay close attention to each and every hour, every second, spent there. Everyone in war hated the jungle, and especially in this war. Even Darby, who never complained about a thing related to the soldier's life, muttered to himself as he slapped at the dizzying variety of invertebrates that assaulted every inch of exposed skin and each orifice in turn. Tiny biting sandflies whined inside ears. Fire ants crawled up legs and backs and necks, spiting acid into pinprick wounds like an army of miniature devils. Leeches, long and thin and reaching out like blind, gasping baby birds, showed up everywhere. And the mosquitoes, always the mosquitoes, the size of houseflies, digging into the flesh to find blood and deposit fevered madness. These were the first enemies of any and all wars, shock troops of the natural world, and every step was another battle in a crusade declared against the arrogant apes a million years ago. The boneless ones would outlive everything else in the kingdom.

Then came the plants and trees, branches whipping faces, thorns cutting hands, and low-lying creepers grabbing at ankles. Walls of bamboo blocking easy trails, each cane twenty feet high and strong as ferry poles. The land did not want men here, and grew things on its surface to keep them out.

The rain was always in the background, coming and going as it pleased, and the mud it created sucked at boots and rotted the feet inside them. Five days in, and everything from the ankle down was either pickled or blistered, silver dollars of skin coming off with drenched socks soaked in blood. Wet feet had lost wars, and this one was no exception.

Mammals didn't even need to join the fray from their perch at the top of the chain. Grunt tales told of wild boars and a rogue tiger occasionally taking scalps from both sides, but they didn't factor in the grand grind of material attrition, only weighing in on occasional nights of specialty death when gibbons in the high branches and muntjac sniffing through the leaves could sound like anything and everything the mind feared.

Whatever the percentage, the combination of the wilderness war machine could lay low a battalion before anyone with guns even showed up. *Animalia* and *Plantae* doing the jab and cross with an unlimited store of energy, and motivation that predated recorded time.

No one with guns showed up in the Laotian jungle for five days, and by the end of the fifth, the rigors of the elements without a clear end game in sight to keep them focused and moving forward wore the men down like spent wind-up toys, the keys in their backs turning one last time before they came to a stop. Chapel felt the exhaustion of the men, and sensed the growing frustration, and called to shut it down for the night an hour earlier than the previous two days. To the men, it felt like a holiday.

They bedded down in what passed for a clearing. Broussard arranged his hooch next to a small alcove in a rock escarpment pushed up from the damp ground, then set out to find Chapel before his body put his mind to sleep. He found him at the far end of camp, tending a fire built in the wet gap of a tangle of huge gray tentacle roots billowing out from a massive Australian fig tree that rose above him, standing vigil. Chapel poked at the flames with a metal rod, watching the sparks jump before being smothered by the damp air. Soldiers didn't see many fires out in the bush, due to lack of dry fuel, concerns about visibility, and a host of more mundane issues, but Chapel had conjured one out of the mud like a gun-barrel wizard. The roots seemed to writhe and move in closer to Chapel as Broussard approached. Tricks of the tired mind. Ruse of the jungle.

"Where's Morganfield?" Broussard said.

"What can I do for you, Specialist Broussard?"

Broussard paused, weighing out a portion of delicacy. "I just wanted to tell you that the men are getting a little…"

Chapel waited for him to continue.

"A little restless."

"They nominate you to come tell me?"

"No, sir."

Chapel ruminated, watching the fire. "I know they are," he said.

"They want to know where we're going."

"I know that, too."

"You going to tell them? Tell us?"

Chapel dug the rod deep into the flames, poking metal into the mud underneath it, striking one of the roots. "Do you like poetry, Specialist Broussard?"

"Some, I guess. Depends."

Chapel smiled, looked off into the complete black of night, and blinked, letting his eyes adjust to the darkness. Then he recited:

> "We sow the glebe, we reap the corn,
> We build the house where we may rest,
> And then, at moments, suddenly,
> We look up to the great wide sky,
> Inquiring wherefore we were born…
> For earnest or for jest?"

Chapel returned his gaze to the fire.

"I think I know that one," Broussard said.

"Do you, now?" Chapel said.

Broussard reached back into his memory to freshman-year English, all that poetry that none of the other boys liked, but he secretly did. Some of it, anyway. He had to read in front of the class, in that northern school, and kids snickered at his accent. He only heard his own voice passing across his ears, not the words moving through his brain, but some of it lingered long enough to be folded up and stored away. He never spoke the same way again after that first day. No Yankee was going to hold anything over him. They were all the same anyway.

"Yeah," Broussard said. "Barrett Browning, right? Elizabeth. That 'sow the glebe' thing stuck with me. Had kind of a 'Jabberwocky' feel."

"Do you remember the ending?"

"No, I don't."

"Shame. It's the best part," Chapel said.

Broussard waited for him to continue, possibly recite the ending of the poem, or give him something to tell the other men, but Chapel offered nothing more, staring into the wizard's fire and digging into the coals with that glowing tip of iron as the roots gathered up closer around him.

Broussard walked back to his hooch while the rest of the men finished their chow, buried their trash, and prepped for sleep. He tumbled the verses over in his mind, but forget the words each time he did. He didn't tell the others that he'd tried to talk to Chapel, and had gotten nowhere. That would add to the discontent, and they were all too far out into the wilderness to start whispering—or shouting—about mutiny. Scared minds need a scapegoat, and if the men decided to hang the hooves on Chapel, with only Morganfield in his corner, things could go south in a hurry, for all of them.

In the camp clearing, carved out from the grass and tangle of soaked plants, Darby was lying on his back in the mud, looking up into the patch of darkened sky through a break in the forest canopy. "I think I'm just going to sleep outside tonight," he said.

"You'll wake up bones when them ants get to you," Render said, pounding in a stake for his hooch with the back of his Ka-Bar.

"Bugs don't like me," Darby said. "I'm too mean."

"Shit," Render said with a chuckle. "You sweet as canned milk, white boy."

McNulty squatted in his stained skivvies, a mirror in his hand, examining his pudgy body and peeling off leeches with the blade of his knife, then burning them with his Zippo. "I got leeches in places I didn't even know I had skin."

"Better watch out that they don't crawl up inside your peckerwood, peckerwood," Render said.

McNulty paled. "They can do that?"

"Don't worry, Chicago," Darby said, his eyes closed, "They don't grow leeches that small."

The other men laughed. McNulty threw a charred leech at Darby.

Medrano was scratching his skin maniacally, leaving red, irritated patches. "Something's been biting me all day. Bunch of things. Driving me crazy."

"Everything bites out here," Render said.

"Different country, same jungle," Broussard said.

"Same war, too," Render said.

"I don't even know what war we're fighting now," McNulty said with a grimace as he pulled off an exceptionally long leech. "They didn't tell us any of this shit in boot camp."

"They don't tell boots shit," Render said, "just what they need to know to *kill, kill, kill*, right? Ooh-rah and all the good Marine bullshit? Nah, man… Nah. They want to keep us dumb, dying young and full of cum with stars in our eyes, you dig? We fighting the war the big bosses tell us to fight. That Chapel's just another one of them big bosses. Star Spangled Banner playing a bugle out his ass."

"He ain't like that," Broussard said.

Render shot him a look. "Man, how do you know?"

Broussard pressed the toe of his boot into the mud, making repeated geometric shapes. "I just do."

"Fuck them big bosses, okay?" Darby said, catching a shooting star arcing across the sky. "I'm fightin' for y'all."

"You just fightin' to fight, with your crazy ass," Render said. "My daddy always told me that white folk can't get enough of war. Can't get enough. Genocide, homicide, land grabbin'..."

"I am who I am," Darby said, scratching at a rash under his armpit. "A monkey with a club."

Medrano chuckled. "Albino monkey."

"We can't all be born perfectly brown, amigo," Darby said. "Like a roasted turkey."

"Our big boss might not know what war we're fighting, either," Render said, glancing over to Chapel's fig tree and the tent now set up where he sat over his fire. No light glowed from inside, like on most nights. He was either asleep, listening in the dark, or gone.

Broussard looked at Render, noticing the nervous way his fingers were pinching and fidgeting.

"We gon fight until we told not to fight no more, and we get sent stateside, either sittin' in a chair or lyin' in a box," Darby said.

"You need to stop saying shit like that," McNulty said.

"I'm just pontificatin' the truth, my Union brother," Darby said. "Believe it or not. The world gon keep spinnin' either way."

McNulty angrily pulled up his pants and threw on his shirt. "That negative shit ain't good for nothin'."

The men sat in uneasy quiet. The air was hot and damp, the jungle oppressively silent, seeming to crowd in close around the camp. Like those roots around Chapel. Tricks and ruses.

"You think we make it out of here?" Medrano said.

"*Shiiit,*" Render said, laughing.

"Why wouldn't we?" Broussard said. The other men looked at him, including Darby, who was sitting up, the entire back part of his body covered in mud. "I don't think we're here to fight," he continued, "Humping these boxes in a small group, traipsin' around God knows where. Did you see what was in those choppers? What kind of fighting are we doing with cable and boxes? Without artillery or air support? Chapel got something else in mind."

"Yeah, but what?" Medrano said.

Broussard shrugged.

"Maybe we bait," Render said.

"Why would we go to so much trouble to be bait in a whole different country?" Broussard said. "Vietnam's full of it. The whole south."

"Maybe we're a sacrifice," McNulty said quietly.

"Now there's a dark thought." Darby smiled. "Didn't think you had it in you, Chicago."

"Maybe the moon smashes into the earth tomorrow," Broussard said. "We keep our heads up, do shit right, and we get out of here. All of us. Doesn't matter what the mission is. We ain't here to give orders. We here to take them, and then get the hell out of this place."

"Look who's the good soldier now," Render said, disgust twisting his face. Broussard ignored him.

"But what are we supposed to do?" Medrano said. "No one's telling us shit, and there's no one to ask out here. Feels like a fucking setup."

"Yeah, I don't know," Render said. "Something don't feel right." He stood and paced, his hands working faster, twitching and gesturing unconsciously. "Man, I hate this shit. All of it. Don't none of us belong out here, all by ourselves, without supporting fire, resupply, chain of command. None of us need to be out here."

"Chapel does," Broussard said, looking over at the man's hooch buried within the roots of the tree.

"He don't neither," Render said. "He don't *belong*, you dig? Ain't none of us *belong* here. We outsiders. We in *their* back yard, like a bunch of stray dogs, and they're getting the shotgun after us."

"Everyone hates it, man," McNulty said. "Not knowing shit. You're not the only one, so stop acting like you always are."

"Hate it?" Render said. "This ain't some *inconvenience*, white boy. This out here is just life for us. Being told what to do without a reason why. Treated like we not important or worthy of any fucking explanation for nothing'. Hating got nothing to do with it."

"Like I said," McNulty added, not offering anything more.

"Oh come on, man," Render said, his voice raising. "I mean, come the fuck *on*. It's different for you chucks. Everything is, no matter where you go, getting that prince treatment, so don't start speaking like you know how it for us, for me and Crayfish."

"Here we go again," McNulty said, rolling his eyes.

"I'm telling you because you need to know. Broussard know. Shit, even Medrano know."

"Yep, I know," Medrano said, combing his hair, blotches of iodine making a stained patchwork on his skin.

"It's different for us," Render said, deflating, sitting on the ground. "It'll always be different. No matter where we are." He roughly wiped tears from his eyes with the back of his hand.

McNulty shook his head and ducked into his hooch. "It's pointless talking to you about anything."

Broussard looked at Darby, who was oddly quiet, sitting cross-legged and rubbing a thin, almost invisible layer of mud over every inch of exposed skin, staring out into the total blackness of the jungle around them. "What about you, Darby?"

"What about what?"

"I don't know," Broussard said, wishing he had a fire of his own, like Chapel did before he doused it without sharing. "About any of it."

"I love it out here," Darby said.

Render sniffed. "What?"

"I love it."

"Love it?" McNulty said from inside his hooch. "Man, you fucking crazy."

"Yeah, that's some jive-ass bullshit right there." Render laughed. "Ain't nobody who's *been* here loves it out here."

"No, I mean it. I really do love it." Darby's voice sounded dreamy, almost childlike as he rubbed his hands over his skin, covering his cheap tattoos and scars with the reddish brown mud that created a protective layer against every biting thing in the wilderness that surrounded them.

Render gritted his teeth, a "*pssshhh*" escaping between them and waved him away.

"What do you love about it?" Broussard asked. He was genuinely curious.

Darby held up his arms, stretching them wide. "The freedom, man. The goddamn freedom of it all. Can't you feel it?"

"That's some pie-in-the-sky bullshit. No one's free out here, motherfucker," Render said, standing up and getting heated. What right did some down-south white boy have to talk about freedom? Freedom for who? "No one," Render said. "On either side. *Any* side."

"No, but we are," Darby said. "All of us are, you just don't realize it. Don't remember it."

"The *fuck*?" Render was beyond incredulous. "Hey Cray, you hearin' this?"

"Out here," Darby continued, "We're human beings as we was supposed to be. Wanderin' the land, fightin', fuckin', killin' each other to survive. That's freedom, brother. That's the freedom of the cave that we left behind and been tryin' to find ever since."

"I ain't your brother, chuck," Render said.

"Yes, you is. We *all* brothers. We don't remember that neither."

Render said nothing, sitting down hard on the ground and staring into the dim lantern that provided the only light in the clearing, tears once again rimming his eyes. Broussard watched Render, worried about him, as Darby continued.

"This is my third tour," he said, completely covered in mud now. "I finished my first, and after I got back home, I signed up again. Second time, they sent me home, callin' me 'emotionally unfit' or some such college-boy garbage. Tried to enlist after that, and got rejected. So I took my cousin's ID—he looks a lot like me, you know—and signed up as him, just before he got drafted anyway. Did both of us a favor. Heck, I should be lance corporal, not a private. But I don't care none. I'm just a soldier."

"What's your cousin's name?" McNulty asked, his head sticking out of his hooch now.

"Tom Darby."

"So, Tim and Tom Darby?" Render said. "And y'all look like twins?"

"Dang close."

Render nudged Broussard's leg. "Ay, I ain't gonna say *nothin'* about keepin' it in the family, okay?"

Darby just shrugged, the mud starting to dry and lighten, cracking when he moved. "They wouldn't allow me to be here, them powers that be, but I had to come back. I need it. I need to be here. I get real restless when I ain't."

"*Pendejo!*"

Everyone looked at Medrano, who dumped his coffee onto the ground. "I could be home with my family, with my wife, my kids, my mom and dad, and they send me back here every time. And *you*, they don't even want you, and you cheat to get sent back over here?"

"Don't be sore, Jorge," Darby said. "This ain't got nothin' to do with you."

"That's some fucking *güero* bullshit, man." Medrano stalked off away from the clearing. "Bullshit!"

"He's gonna get into them leeches out there," McNulty said.

"Didn't mean to make him sore," Darby said, watching Medrano go. "Got nothin' to do with him."

"He'll be all right," Broussard said. "Just misses home."

"I get that, I guess," Darby said. "I try to, anyway. But I don't miss home. Nothin' there for me to miss. Job in the textile mill, I guess. Maybe do some farm work, scoop horseshit or some such. But when I got home, the last time, hell *every* time, I looked around, and the buildings and stores and the people and even the trees—everything looked faded out. Drained of color like an old shirt that been washed too many times. Trees even. Ain't that somethin'? The trees back home didn't look green no more. They looked gray. Everything looked gray." Darby looked out into the night, sending his mind back home, to the trees of his youth, trying to conjure them up lush and emerald out of the gray. A pair of bloodshot white eyeballs looking out through a layer of dried mud. "Everything's green here."

Leaves whispered at the edge of the jungle. Quick feet disturbed the underbrush. The men scrambled for their rifles.

"It's me," Morganfield whispered, walking briskly into the clearing. "Let's move."

"Where're we going?" Broussard said.

"Top of the ridgeline," Morganfield said, checking his sidearm.

"Why?" McNulty said, standing outside of his hooch.

"Chapel's there," Morganfield said. "He's seen it."

"Seen what? Gookers?"

He was gone, back into the jungle. The men looked at each other, then hopped to their feet, grabbing their rifles, ammo, and gear, pulling on helmets and boonie hats and leaving their packs behind. McNulty was shaking, muttering a prayer under his breath. Darby laughed as he got up, pulling on his fatigues over the dirt covering his skin.

## Chapter Twenty-Five

## Burn Then the River Down

The men clambered through the undergrowth after Morganfield, breathing hard and sweating under their hastily assembled gear, following his disappearing trail through the jungle, the ground rising in a sharp incline.

The thick crush of vegetation broke and the men found themselves on a wide grassy rim that sloped down into a gentle open valley, lit blue-bright by a full moon. Away from the jungle, heading up into the mountains, massive blocks of granite were stacked and clustered like the ruins of a toy castle, foam bricks scattered by a brat god in a fit of rage or boredom.

On the far side of the valley were two nearly identical mountain peaks that might have been a singular edifice at some point in some forgotten epoch, before the patient wear of water cut a V between them, cleaving one giant child of the earth into begrudging twins. What remained of this tributary was a gentle river that now flowed between them, creating the valley and moving on to the south of the country without a single memory of what it had done in times long past.

The men stared down at this basin, a pastoral scene too perfect to not be suspect, and gripped their rifles tight, waiting for a sign of the enemy. Broussard was excited and terrified, not necessarily about fighting, but what he would do when it was time to fight. That old fear, whispering to him from the playground and the street corner, the barroom and the battlefield. Inflict pain or take it. Both equally horrifying to him. Embarrassing in the action and the reaction. He felt like he knew what he'd do this time, but there were no guarantees when war cries filled the air, the steel flashed, and gunpowder started to burn.

"I don't see noth—"

Morganfield grabbed McNulty by the back of his shirt and yanked him to the ground, his helmet falling off his head.

"Keep your heads down, goddamn it," Chapel whispered, now among them again. No one heard him approach. "There's eyes everywhere."

"Whose eyes?" McNulty mashed his helmet back on and wiped mud from his face, shooting Morganfield a hateful glare.

Chapel didn't answer, peering intently out into the darkness of the valley below. The gray of his eyes sparked blue, catching the moonlight that somehow added color to them when it leeched it away from everything else.

"What is it, sir?" McNulty said, moving his head back and forth, trying to see what wasn't seeable. Not with his eyes.

"There," he said, pointing between the peaks. "It's going to come from there. Where the twins meet."

"What is?" Broussard couldn't stand the anticipation, suddenly irritated with Chapel's cryptic way of expressing himself when direct facts were desperately needed.

"Watch," Chapel said.

Broussard did, focusing his gaze on the intersection point of the two mountains. He saw nothing at first, then noticed a faint, reddish glow at the bottom of the V, like a thin artery of warm blood coming to life inside a dead heart. The darkness all around and down below took a breath and stood up, moving higher, pushed by a strand of light that made its way down a dip in the shallow valley.

The first head of flame emerged and slowly descended. It was the River, lit on the surface by fire. Not one tongue of flame, but a hundred, then a thousand, tens of thousands of tiny rafts carrying passengers of light from the mountain country beyond down into a channel plain on a placid current. Lanterns, shrines, dotted with flickering candles. Together, they made a River ablaze.

"What kind of shit is this?" McNulty said.

"Beautiful," Darby breathed, full of awe. "Goddamn beautiful."

Broussard looked at Chapel, who felt his eyes and looked back. His white teeth were gleaming in the moonlight. "We found it, Broussard."

The men looked at each other, brows furrowed, shrugs of confusion curling up their faces.

"Tonight, gentlemen," Chapel said.

## Chapter Twenty-Six

### Anniversary

I fix up on the foot-wide lip of concrete separating the mud and humanity of the Floating City from the dead water down below. It's only a quarter vial of half 'n half, but it feeds all the empty spaces inside me drained hollow by the horrors of the French house. I toss the spike and dangle my legs above the canal and watch the parade of plastic drift by.

My mind revs as my body unwinds, and I try to process what I just witnessed and heard, and what I know I must do, but I'm pressed by the smell of this water, landlocked and tainted, itching to get out to sea and purge itself. The sheer stink of it, this ruined stuff. It'll never get out of my nostrils, never leave my hair, my pores. If I ever escape this place, am somehow pulled from it kicking and screaming and weeping with benediction, I don't think I'll ever stop smelling it. I've never gotten used to it, and know that I will never stop smelling it. I try to remember the perfume of Louisiana, the flowers and grass, the smell of its own brand of brackish water, but I can't. All of that died inside my nose a long time ago.

Plastic bottles and bags move below me. A rubber bicycle tire looking like a black snake eating its tail. Chunks of pink insulation. A child's sock and a naked, armless dolly, wide blue eyes staring sightlessly at the darkening sky. The lid of a large container, heaped with wet market flowers and dotted with dripping candles, burning brightly amid the dreary trash.

I look upstream in the canal, and see more tiny teeth of flame flickering in the dying daylight. An armada of little shrines, drifting on a sluggish current. I can see them clearly this time, as close as I am, even in my speedball haze. Get their details. Two glass cats with a candle between them on a raft made of mismatched lengths of bamboo. A framed picture of a smiling North Vietnamese Army officer, distinguished in his jacket and hat. More pictures of other men, some of women, some of children. Each one died away from their home, their earthly remains never recovered. This was why the girl didn't leave the house with me, why she wouldn't let me pay her back. She didn't take me to the French house to help me, she did it to help the one I killed, one of so many who inspired the construction of each tiny shrine, launched into rivers, streams, and the putrid water of the Floating City.

It was an anniversary, and the girl knew it. The River was burning again for all of the wandering souls, set on their uninvited journeys by men just like me.

Time for this one to go.

## Chapter Twenty-Seven

## A Love of Shared Disasters

Back in a chair, waiting outside of a door. Chairs and waiting near killed me, and might kill me yet. We'll see how this goes.

Nothing followed me inside, from this world or any other. Black Shuck has never been here, and for the first time, I wonder why. I'm wondering a lot of things for the first time today, after my time in the French house, after getting gamed by the girl who made me feel like a hero just long enough to matter. But looking back, I've never felt the presence of anything in this place other than that of the general and the men, women, and children under his employ, who all make up a giant octopus with many tentacles, great and small, grasping and crushing whatever they can find.

Phuong appears in the hallway, her face hard as ever. She's the hardest person I know. She served in the war. Fought, I should say, as no one "served" on their side, as it was a given. No service required, as much as breathing and smiling isn't a service. She did serve the general, then as she does now, and rose to his right hand, being brilliant and ruthless and madly efficient in the killing of Americans. Once the general died, or was killed, or snatched up in the middle of the night by the Americans that they didn't have a chance to kill, she'd take over.

I smile at her, and Phuong breaks that warlord mask and smiles back, the only one around here who does. "*Brou*-ssard," she says, as well as she can. She learned my name, practiced it, the only one around here who did. I'd allow myself to think that she liked me, maybe even more than liked, but that would more than likely get me killed. Instead, I take it for what I probably is—general politeness in the workplace—and leave it at that.

Phuong gestures down the hallway, to the big reinforced-steel door at the end of it. I'm here for my next commission, which isn't out of the ordinary. That it will be my last most definitely is. I'm not here for business today, I'm here for barter, and certainly not with the general. I'm taking notes, and making lists, and will leave Phuong off of them, because I know that the business of the general will always continue, no matter who is conducting it, as nature and the nature of crime and man's failings abhors a vacuum. When it all goes down, and Uncle Sam kicks down the big reinforced-steel door of One Time Uncle Charlie and mashes faces and shoots holes in the brittle old guard, Phuong will wear the gold bars, and maybe, *maybe*, all of the places touched by all the arms of the octopus general will be just a little bit better off. The way I reckon, if every king was a queen, there would be far less tears in this world.

I get up and walk down the hall, Phuong letting me pass and following behind, her steps silent, just like she learned moving swiftly through the jungle from the time she was a teenager, scared and angry and learning how to make her mask. She killed so many of mine because mine killed so many of hers first. Give and take and then take some more. Motherfucking tug-of-war.

I reach the door and knock the required number of times, and it opens up before me. I step inside, one last time.

*T. E. GRAU*

## Chapter Twenty-Eight

## Spook Money

The joint is mostly deserted as I take a seat at the bar, perching up on a wobbly stool. The boonie hat fits loose on my clean-shaven head. Back in the war, I let my hair grow out as much as I was allowed, making me feel taller. Today, right now, I wanted to feel sleek and fast, able to knife through anything.

The bartender walks over and looks at me with an implacable expression that he either practiced or earned the hard way. He's never said a word to me in the five years I've been coming here. I don't think I've ever heard his voice. He raises his eyebrows and waits.

I ask for water. His eyebrows bunch into a furrow of genuine confusion, the most expression I've ever gotten from the guy. I don't add anything to my order, so he shrugs, and gestures with his chin before walking off to fetch a glass.

I look down the bar, and the man is sitting on the corner stool. I didn't see him when I sat down. Fucking spooks.

He checks out my weekend fatigues. "You going to war?"

I rub the horseshoe outline in the pocket of my trousers, surrounding three plastic baggies filled with medicine in a protective semicircle. Not exactly military issue, these pants, but sturdy. New ones, purchased just for the occasion at what passes for an Army surplus in Bangkok, selling war supplies creatively re-routed a decade back by enterprising quartermasters who only wrote in pencil and kept their stock binders loose.

"I think so," I say.

The bartender brings my glass of water and sets in front of me. He drops a lime into it, gives me the smallest grin, then walks away. It's a day of firsts.

"What brings you here," the man says, "Other than the quality of the tap water?"

"I got something for you."

"Oh?" he says, actually surprised.

I take my hat off and rub my head. I'm sweating, and not from the heat. I'm trying to get my mind right, and the chemicals are leaking from my body, clearing up room for a fresh shipment from the shelf of the general that'll certainly be my last. A day of firsts and lasts.

"Nice haircut," he says.

I ignore him. "I'm not writing anything down, and I'm not signing anything. I'll tell you what I know, and it's up to you to do with it what you want."

"Okay," he says.

"And then I want that favor you were talking about."

The man looks at my glass, then at the bruises and cuts on my face. "You quit drinking?"

I touch the glass, then adjust the wound in my side, wincing. "Yeah."

"I hope it was nothing I did."

"Can we talk about that favor, or what?"

"Depends on what we talk about before that."

I look around. "You got any place more private?"

He gestures to a booth in the back of the bar, a location normally reserved for five-dollar blowjobs and cheap street gangsters, or often some combination of the two. Seems fitting, somehow. I get up slowly, favoring my side, and walk deeper into the shadows of the place.

I haven't said anything for two full minutes, and he's still scribbling in his little notepad. Finally, he underlines something three times, clicks his pen and stows it inside his jacket pocket.

"Well, I've got to say," he says with a grin, "you're either very connected, or very nosy."

"I prefer 'observant.' A machine ain't too complicated when you look at it from the inside, where all the wiring is."

"Well said. At any rate, this should keep me busy for a while. Thank you, Mr. Broussard."

"It's Specialist Broussard."

A smile plays across his thin lips. That pallid face is waxy as ever. "Yes, of course it is."

I point to the notebook on the table, resting under a protective hand. "Does that earn me a favor?"

"I'd say it does."

"Anything I want?"

"No, certainly not. I'm not a fucking genie. Something within reason, of course."

"Okay..." I take a deep breath, coming in ragged, blowing out cold. My hands are shaking again, atoms in motion. I need to back down off the shit slowly, because I know I can't get through the day like this. Forget about the night, and what always happens then. It's the nights that got me started in the first place. "I need you to find some coordinates for me."

"Oh?"

"They're in Laos. A ridge above a river valley cutting through two symmetrical peaks. About five days hump from a place called the Plain of Jars."

"Well, that sounds perfectly simple." He grinned with those thin lips. This was sarcasm, and it didn't come naturally to the man.

"Check Operation Algernon."

The man writes this down. "Any name to cross reference?"

I haven't said it for five years. Maybe longer, now. But it's always on the tip of my tongue, dancing to get out. Finally, I let it. "Augustus Chapel."

"Branch?"

"I don't know. Your branch."

"I don't have a branch."

I nod. "Neither did he."

The man nods. "I'll see what I can do." He stands, slipping his notebook inside his jacket, rejoining the pen. I get to my feet, shaking the whole way, holding my side. "You okay?" he says.

"I don't know."

"You need a lift home? I can send someone…"

"No. I'm not going home."

"You got a place to stay?"

I shrug. I'm not really sure. Doesn't matter either way at this point.

"Meet me back here tomorrow. Same time. I'll know by then if I can help you. If I can't, we'll see about doing you a different favor."

"If you can't, I won't need a different one."

He doesn't understand this. I honestly don't either, but my mouth said it, and I'm going to take it at its word, as my body doesn't seem to be working in unison with my head anymore. I'll let instinct guide me from here on out.

The man pats the notebook inside his jacket. "Thank you for this. It'll do a lot of good." He holds out his hand.

"I'd like to believe that, but I don't," I say. The man's smile wavers just the slightest bit. "Call it professional skepticism," I say, taking his hand and shaking it. It's a small hand, but firm.

The man nods. "Fair enough." He releases my hand. "Tomorrow, then."

"Tomorrow."

## Chapter Twenty-Nine

## (Four) Seeds of the Pomegranate

The vibration of the helicopter is different than what I remember, the roar of the engines softer. Less rattling and wind. Maybe it's the machine itself, but maybe it's just me. I'm different, too. Smaller, but harder, like the man's hand. None of it feels the same, or remotely right.

Maybe it's because I'm getting sick. Sicker. I can feel the bugs poking out from their cocoons in my elbows and knees, ready to start their march up and down my arms and legs, fester in my lower back, spit poison into my stomach. I didn't fix enough before I left, and didn't bring enough with me for the long term. Just whatever I had in my pocket, which put me in ration mode, because someone or something had set fire to the cave. I watched from the street as it burned, catching the other buildings next to it, which went up like the cheap props they were. Paper-thin structures built only for the illusion of house and home. People all around me ran and screamed and ran and screamed. It looked like a napalm dance, back in the day. Running and screaming, holding hands to heads, eyes wide, mouths wider. I might have set the fire. I might have. The River might have, too. Shrines on parade, tiny torches in the paws of ceramic cats. I can't remember, but my hands did smell like gasoline, but they always smelled like something that could burn.

That's all behind me now. A five-year yesterday back in Bangkok, the city that collected me from the drain as I sluiced down the trough, picking me up to wait out a sentence of terror and sleepless nights, shot up with chemicals to keep a cosmic hound from coming to steal my air and kill me and take me away to the void. I wonder if Black Shuck was inside, waiting for me, when the first licks of flame carved through the walls, destroying its favorite doghouse where the wall met the ceiling.

I vomit on the steel floor of the chopper. The pilot doesn't turn around, nor does the man from the bar, whose face I can't see. Professional courtesy, I suspect. Just like Phuong, and maybe with the same temperature of low-level loathing. Nothing exists to spooks, not even themselves, and here I am out to find King Spook, living far far underground in his castle in Hades. Will he exist? Did he ever? Where the fuck am I? God lord, am I sick…

The chopper banks suddenly. I pitch to the side and vomit again, the bugs applauding inside me. I might die out here in the jungle without a bullet being fired.

The applause twists into a buzzing, and the sound of water. That old familiar reverberation, fueled by the natural laws and older than the land. The firstborn baby on this dumb spinning rock. The rush of the River gets louder, flooding the engines and slowing the spinning of the X above my head.

With my eyes closed, I can see the blur of green rushing below me like a limitless River as the sound rises up with the water, deafening. With my eyes closed, I can see Black Shuck running on top of the jungle canopy, taking great, bounding leaps at a leisurely but impossible speed. The helicopter is a small, defenseless bird just a little ways ahead and slightly above.

Black Shuck leaps with the sound of a roaring River, exploding into a cresting wave that engulfs the chopper and pulls me back into the water, swallowed up by the current.

## Chapter Thirty-One

## The Ghosts Will Come For You

By the time the men struck camp the next morning and headed up to the ridgeline above the valley, the Hmong were already there, cracking open crates with great efficiency and very little sound, removing sturdy black cabinets, cables, rope, poles, industrial-size battery packs, and other delicate contrivances that seemed at odds with the rough surroundings. Judging by the treatment of the boxes and packaging, and the remnants of it disappearing into the jungle as if by a line of giant leafcutter ants, it looked like there was no plan to take any of the equipment back with the group.

Chapel walked among the tribesmen, exhorting them in their native tongue. Morganfield walked just behind Chapel, calculating figures on a clipboard and whispering suggestions, noting corrections.

The American soldiers were instructed to provide cover, rifles up, scanning every direction in complete confusion as to what was going on.

"Stay sharp," Chapel said, moving over to the troops. "We have nine hours 'til sundown."

"We staying out here for nine hours?" Medrano said.

"I hope you got your beauty sleep last night, Medrano."

"I didn't," Medrano said with a frown, thinking of his comb and mirror.

"What happens then?" Render said.

"When?" Chapel said.

"Sundown."

"Everything," Chapel said.

The men exchanged looks.

"No sleep?" Broussard said.

Chapel turned to him. "Pardon me, Specialist?"

"I mean, we're not going to rest, to sleep?"

"Not tonight. You can sleep for the rest of your life. For the next eighteen hours, we do our work, and hope they don't sleep either."

"Who's they?" Medrano said.

"The fucking lollipop guild, Medrano," Morganfield said, writing figures on his clipboard.

"Hey, fuck you, man."

"Keep your voices down," Chapel said in a hushed tone, before walking back to the Hmong. He was edgy, tense. The men felt it.

"I was just asking," Medrano said to Render. "Why he got to talk to me that way?"

"Spooks gonna spook," Render said.

Medrano shook his head and readjusted the rifle in his hand, muttering curses in Spanish.

McNulty was the closest of the fire team to the tree line, where the Hmong were hoisting the square cabinets into the lowest, thickest branches and lashing them tight, black circles inside each meshed cube facing out toward the valley.

"Speakers?" McNulty said, pushing up the front of his helmet with his index finger. "Why the fuck did we bring speakers way out here? We doing a Sunday school broadcast for the heathen commies?"

"Did he say speakers?" Render asked Broussard.

"Maybe we having a concert," Darby said. "Invite in all of the out-of-towners, show 'em some good ol' American pie, and blast them to ever lovin' Jesus."

"In the middle of a fucking forest?" McNulty said.

"Jungle Woodstock," Broussard said.

"With no stinkin' hippies," Medrano said.

"Maybe the fight comes to us," Render said. "Maybe it's on its way right fucking now, and this is some sort of…protection or something."

"Forcefield," Medrano said, nodding sagely, thinking back to his comic books.

"How would that make sense?" Broussard said to Render.

"What out here *make* sense, Cray?" Render said. "This ain't regular military. This all *irregular*, you dig? I don't know, man… We caught up in something weird."

"You see those two mountains?" Morganfield said, walking up to the soldiers.

Everyone looked at the twin peaks, through which that burning river flowed the night before.

"A good portion of the entire 276th Regiment is holed up just behind that ridge and in the next valley," Morganfield said with a casualness normally reserved for a breakfast order.

"Holy shit." Render brought his rifle to his shoulder and ducked down.

"Righteous," Darby said with a grin.

"There's a thousand gooks behind them mountains?" McNulty's voice rose an octave.

"How do you know that?" Render asked.

"Because that's what we do," Morganfield said. "Know."

"A *thousand* fucking gooks?" McNulty was nearly screaming.

"Give or take a dozen," Chapel said, rejoining the group. "And keep your voice down.."

"Sir!" McNulty said, moving quickly toward Chapel, who frowned at him. McNulty lowered his voice. "Sir, I-I don't mean to overstep, but—"

"Every step you make is an overstep, PV2," Chapel said.

McNulty swallowed that, which made his face flush. "Be that as it may, sir, but the gooners don't have a 276th Regiment. 274th and 275th, but there's no such thing as the 276th."

Render looked at Broussard, genuinely impressed with McNulty for the first time since they'd met.

"Are you through?" Chapel said.

"Yes, sir," McNulty said. "I guess I am."

"Okay, now that you're finished with the primer on formation classification of the Democratic Republic of Vietnam, please allow me to report, Private Second Class McNulty, that extra-agency recon has discovered that along the back side of the ridge and dug in over in the next valley is the 276th Regiment of the NVA." He glared at McNulty, who found something interesting about his boots at that very moment. "This fun group of well rested and fully outfitted boy scouts are planning on joining their brothers and sisters in the fight against the United States military and our ARVN allies as soon as they breach the border, which they will in a matter of days, just in time for Tet. Remember Tet, gentlemen? Do all of you here remember Tet?"

The men nodded, each recalling in their own way the Tet Offensive three years prior in '68, when eighty thousand NVA struck a hundred targets simultaneously, killing four thousand Americans in a matter of days. It was a blitzkrieg of slaughter.

"We're not going to let that happen again," Chapel said. "*Ever.* We're out here to win this goddamn thing, on their turf, taking the fight to the heart of where the enemy finds care and comfort. We're bringing the horror to their bedrooms, bathrooms, war rooms, and hospitals."

The group was quiet, processing this.

"Sir?" Broussard said to Chapel.

"Yes?"

"I think it's time you told us why we're out here. Specifically."

Chapel took a deep breath and exhaled, then nodded to Morganfield, who approached with a round steel canister, painted bright red. He set it on the ground, opened it, and from inside lifted out a recording reel and held it up for view. "Gentlemen, we are here to deliver this."

"What is that?" McNulty said.

"Magnetic audio tape," Morganfield said.

"We gonna play them some good ol' country music," McNulty said, "and blow their zip minds?"

"This is most certainly not a music tape," Morganfield said. Chapel was silent, arms crossed across his chest, watching everyone's reactions.

"See, country ain't music," Render said to McNulty. "I told you, dummy."

"What's on that tape, sir?" Broussard said.

Chapel didn't answer. Still working the process. Gathering intel.

Broussard clenched his jaw and two fists, fighting back anger, frustration, and the sickening ball of fear that had been growing in the pit of his stomach for days. He pointed a finger at Chapel. It shook as it jabbed at the pale face standing across from him. "You tell us, goddamn it. You tell us just what the fuck we're doing out here, and why you marched five strangers across the border to feed us to a thousand VC waiting behind a mountain." Broussard was breathing hard. He was scared, but the fear made him feel strong. Standing this close to the unknown, without a tether, he had nothing to lose.

The men were surprised, and by the identical look each of them fixed on Chapel, for the first time in the entire operation, they seemed to be standing as one single unit.

Chapel nodded, as if waiting for this, and seemed to fight back a smile. "Okay," he said. "Okay then." He unlocked his arms and motioned the group forward. "Come close, gentlemen."

The men formed into a tight semicircle, Broussard the last to join.

Chapel regarded each face in turn. "I don't work for the United States

Army. Not anymore."

None of the men seemed particularly surprised, but finally hearing it aloud did stir something in each of them akin to anxious wonder. They were all now officially off the books, with everything that carried with it.

"But I do still serve my country, running my own PSYOPS department."

"See, I knew it," Render said. "Boss a spook!"

"I wouldn't necessarily call me a spook," Chapel said seriously, then smiled. "But now that I think about it, that *is* the nature of our mission."

The men laughed nervously.

"Some background," Chapel said. "We've known for years that the VC were moving from Vietnam into Laos to lick their wounds, retrain, and generally arm themselves to the eyeteeth with the latest and greatest Chinese hardware to roll off the factory floors of Shanghai. But Laos is Laos, and subject to sovereignty that takes them outside our theater of war, and therefore outside of our official rules of engagement. So naturally we've sent no troops to chase down Charlie other than those flying American aircraft in an attempt to bomb these bastards back to the Pre-Cambrian Age. This, of course, didn't work, as air power is messy and is about as precise as firing a shotgun to kill a spider, and the majority of our unconfirmed but easily assumed kills were civilians whose relatives then took up arms to fight with our enemy against the monsters who dropped fire from the sky on an unengaged populace. Because of this, more unusual measures were needed, and not necessarily those condoned by the government or the military brass of the United States."

"This is an illegal mission?" McNulty said.

"Give the man a cigar!" Render said.

"What about killing another human being *is* legal to you, Chicago?" Darby said.

Chapel held up the tape. "Gentlemen, we are out here to relay a message to the 276th Regiment, and this," he tapped the reel with his finger. "This is our message."

"What is it?"

"You'll see soon enough."

"Don't you mean hear," Broussard said.

"No, you'll see."

"When?" McNulty said.

"Sundown," Chapel said, walking away from the men. "When the ghosts come for us all."

## Chapter Thirty-One

## Somewhere Along the Highway

"Wake up, Broussard."

I'm dreaming, because I've heard that before. I'm in an aquarium inside a jeep rumbling through a river of mud.

"Wake up, Broussard."

I'm flying over the jungle, and Chapel's in the other chopper, looking out into the night, directing without a map.

"Wake up, Broussard."

It's the man from the bar. He's wearing sunglasses and standing on the ground outside the open fuselage door. Below those blacked out lenses, his teeth peer out from between his thin lips, and laugh at me, each tooth in turn. "I thought I lost you there for a second."

I wipe off my mouth and sit up, the reality of everything slowly sinking back into me. I'm sick as shit.

"What's happening?" I say.

"We're here," he says.

He helps me get out of the chopper and stand on smooth grass, feeling for my legs and taking it on faith that they're down there. Everything around me looks just like it did before, but I recognize nothing. I don't know where I am.

The man stands in front of me, and hands me something. I take the object and look down at it.

"What's this?" I ask.

"What do you think it is?"

I hold it out at arm's length, pointed at his forehead. "I remember now," I say.

"You going to be all right?" he says, not the least bit thrown by the .45 caliber barrel pressed against his forehead.

"I don't know."

He raises his eyebrows up over his sunglasses and waits. I lower the gun, and scratch absently at my face with it.

"Which way?" I say.

The man turns and points to a hillside, the tall grass blowing in the slight breeze. "Follow the trail."

"I don't see one."

"You will. When you get close enough." He looks at me, noting the vomit on my clothes, the slack of my jaw. "You going to make it out here?"

"Not really."

He nods. "Retirement withdrawal."

I shiver, feeling cold from the inside out.

"Take care of yourself, Broussard," he says before heading back to the chopper.

"I will."

"And thanks for what you've done. For your country. And for, well…"

He doesn't finish, because he doesn't have to. We both know it's bullshit, all of it everywhere, and only about cashing checks on each and every side.

"I wish I could promise a ride back, but…" He lets that hang there, too, to make sure I know exactly where we stand. "We were never here in the first place." Good little soldier.

"Thanks for the ride," I say, and shoulder my pack.

The man nods, climbs back inside the cockpit, and closes the door. The blades begin to spin, whipping up its own private hurricane that nearly sends me airborne. The chopper ascends into the sky and is gone, the departure echoing off the granite faces that stare down at our silly drama with disinterest. None of us wave goodbye.

I walk toward the tall grass, and without much of a search, I find a worn patch of ground, leading up into the hill country, lorded over by mountains ringed in a beard of silken white clouds.

I part the grass and touch feet to trail. The green closes in behind me, as if I was never here.

## Chapter Thirty-Two

### *Retour du Fantôme*

There's something in these trees, hiding under the water of the rice paddies. Something closing in on me, and it's not Black Shuck. It's something worse.

The foot trail winds, and takes me through flooded fields and lakes coated with lily pads and legions of dragonflies. Flowers smell of perfume, and the wet air keeps it close to the ground. The pathway cuts up terraces and across narrow bridges built for one traveler at a time. This is ancient country, and it watches me, whispering messages to the things in the trees and under the water. I'm thirsty, but I dare not drink anything out here. Something will climb inside me if I do.

After what could be days but is probably only hours, I walk up a hillside on a narrow but precisely cut and hard-packed trail that zigzags up the incline through a series of switchbacks. The trail wasn't noticeable from below, expertly disguised by low growing foliage lining the track. You'd only find it if you were on the path.

I climb the hill, sweating and spent, and find a mini-plateau that seems to be cut right out of the side of the mountain. The land is smooth clay the color of polished rust, supporting a compact village of sturdy Hmong huts. Each dwelling is raised on stilts, with a small porch protected by a railing of thick bamboo, and a set of steps leading to the ground. In my fever, I can vaguely recall bayou shacks, hovering over the swamp or occasionally dry land that quickly regresses into marsh with each heavy rain. Laos always did remind me of Louisiana, but for some reason Vietnam never did. Bangkok reminded me of nothing I'd ever seen before, or wanted to see again. But Laos always carried a hint of home, and filled me with a mix of strange longing.

I look up and down at the precisely arranged rows of houses, six on each side of the central clearing. It looks like military housing. The porch of the last house at the far end creaks under a heavy weight. I glance down, and see a great black shape sitting patiently just above the small staircase. Black Shuck stares back at me, its expression unreadable. It traveled ahead, knowing where I'd end up. It was no longer chasing, but waiting. For some reason, I'm not scared.

A man emerges from the largest hut and leans forward on the bamboo railing. He's old and gaunt, deeply tanned skin covering tight muscle and knobby bones. Sandy white eyebrows furrow down low over far grayer eyes, now sunk deeper into the additional lines covering his skull, marking his days like thin cuts in a cracked leather belt. But those eyes shine like they know that secret still.

It's Chapel.

I open my dry mouth to recite the words I'd committed to memory after tracking down the book for months. Once I finally laid my hands and my eyes on it, I burned those words, that ending, into my mind. I never knew if I'd have a reason to speak them aloud, but I never knew anything about my life since I left the bayou.

> *"And sometimes through life's heavy swound*
> *We grope for them!—with strangled breath*
> *We stretch our hands abroad and try*
> *To reach them in our agony—*
> *And widen, so, the broad life-wound*

*Which soon is large enough for death."*

Chapel grins, something genuine and filled with just a touch of proud surprise. "You knew the ending after all," he says, his voice a note lower, but still clear and strong.

"No, I had to learn it," I say.

Chapel nods slowly. He always knew what I was saying even when I didn't come out and say it.

"What are you doing out here?" I say.

"I could ask you the same."

I shake my head, and take a step forward. Shaky now. Always shaky. I'm not sure how far I should go. Not sure how he feels, or how I do. Hmong tribesmen, dressed in civvy clothes, are posted up all over the clearing, Chinese-made AK-47s resting over shoulders and in the crook of tanned arms. The spook's army. He collects one everywhere he goes.

Chapel steps down from he porch, walks up and wraps his arms around my shoulders, bringing me in for a tight hug. Still strong. I press one arm around the man's back, then grimace. Chapel releases me.

"You hurt?"

"Nothing major."

Chapel nods. "Let me get a look at you." Sharp gray irises inspect my face, then pull down his brow into a furrow. "Your eyes," he says.

"Different now."

"Yes they are." He appraises me again. "Come inside."

"Do you see it?"

Chapel glances at me. I gesture to the last house in the village. Nothing is there.

"Come on inside," Chapel says, taking me by the shoulder.

I walk with him into the hut, but not as the good soldier entering the bunker, but as the hunter entering the den of my prey. I'm not sure if Chapel knows this, and don't care. He'll find out soon enough.

## Chapter Thirty-Three

## Rest Home for Wandering Souls

I'm seated on the ground, a cup of tea and a platter of fruit in front of me. Mangos, papaya, dragon fruit, wild haired rambutans, and a single orange the size of a grapefruit. I wonder about that orange, just for a second, but then realize that there would be no way he'd know. I finish a pitcher of water in one long gulp, which makes me feel sicker and just as thirsty.

A Hmong woman and a man stand in front of me, with various children clinging to their legs and peeking out at me. The adults are glaring, the children just stare. One of them makes a face at me, rolling his eyes into his head and showing his lower teeth. Chapel returns from the other room with a bowl of steaming rice, spiced with curry and lemongrass. He places this on the table, dusts off his hands, and clears his throat.

"That's Sua, my brother in law," Chapel says, gesturing to the man, then to the woman. "And this is Maiv, my wife." He speaks to them in Hmong, and I detect my name.

Sua nods his head slightly. Maiv stares at me, the disgust in her eyes dripping down and slightly twisting the forced inscrutability of her expression. It always comes down to the eyes.

"The children?" I say.

"What about them?" Chapel says.

I don't say anything.

Their obligation to manners at an end, Maiv turns a glance to Chapel, then slips out of the room, Sua and the children in tow.

Chapel watches her go. "She doesn't like you."

"She prejudiced too?"

"Isn't everybody?"

I don't feel like having this talk. I didn't come out here to have this talk. I should have kept my mouth shut.

"She thinks you're going to take me away from here," he says. "Take me back to where I came from."

"I'm not taking anyone anywhere. I ain't like you."

"Yeah, you are," he says. "That's why you're here."

I can't tell if he's implying that I'm going to take him somewhere, or that I'm like him. Either way, he's wrong.

He watches me struggle inside, still gathering intel. In the dim light of the hut, without the squint, his wrinkles that once looked so proud and distinguished now just make him look worn out. Tired.

"I'm here…" I shake my head, stand up and pull the pistol from my waistband, point it at his face. "I'm here to get some answers. Where you go after that is up to you."

"You don't need to hold a gun on me," Chapel says mildly. He seems neither surprised nor distressed. "I'll tell you everything you want to know."

"I do need to hold a gun on you, so you know what it feels like."

"You don't think I know?"

"Not lately. Not living out here, like this."

"Put the gun away, Broussard."

"I ain't—"

"Put the gun away, or you'll be cut down where you stand." Chapel nods to various corners of the hut. In each one, a rifle barrel pokes into the room. I never saw them, certainly didn't hear them. I guess Chapel always rolls with ghosts.

"They gonna shoot?"

"Keep that gun in my face for another six or seven seconds and they will."

"Call 'em off."

"They won't listen to me."

"Why not?"

"Because I'm not in charge here."

I hear several safety latches click to the "off" position.

"Bullshit."

Chapel shrugs. "Okay."

My new eyes can see fingers tightening on triggers. I lower the pistol, then stuff it into the back waistband of my trousers. I look to each corner. The barrels are gone, as silently as they appeared. No shadow has replaced them. Not yet. That would be coming along shortly, sure as rain in the jungle. No way in hell Black Shuck is still on that porch. It'll want to see what's happening in here.

"Sit?" Chapel says.

"You giving me orders?" I say. "You think you're my daddy? 'Cause you sure as shit ain't my commanding officer."

"Will you please sit?" Chapel says, his tone unchanged.

I hesitate, wanting to protest, wanting to shoot this motherfucker, let him feel my rage and hurt at being lured into the jungles of Laos to die with brothers that I barely knew, didn't have time to know, for a cause that was madness from the inside out, but I don't know how to say what I want to say, and don't have a weapon in my hand, so I sit. I sink down two inches in the low rattan chair. I get up and move it aside, then sit on the floor, thinking about peeling the orange that's in front of me.

Chapel joins me on the ground, crossing his legs under him with some effort and a series of pops from creaky tendons. The sounds stab through the buzzing in my brain, as the River begins to reach out again, finding me here in Chapel's hut. Always finding me, forever and ever and ever.

"So," Chapel says, his voice barely audible over the sound of the water now rushing around me. Black Shuck fills the doorway behind him, cutting off the light from outside. The hound doesn't come into the room, because it doesn't have to, not with the water flooding the floor. "Where do we go from here?"

## Chapter Thirty-Four

## Orphans from a Different Tribe

Broussard sat cross-legged in front of his hooch, shaking off a feeling of falling, or being pulled fast down a great black hillside. He might have dozed off, but he wasn't sure. He hadn't slept well since crossing over into Laos, haunted with queer dreams.

He looked over at Darby, who was reassembling his M-14 in the dying light of day aided by a kerosene lantern, oiling each part and metal surface and buffing it with a small stained rag.

"It's gonna be sundown soon, and then..." Darby said, sensing that Broussard was awake and watching him.

"Yeah," Broussard said. "And then."

"Why ain't you sleepin'?"

"I don't know. I'm starting to forget how."

"You always the first one sleepin,'" Darby said with a chuckle. "Sleep through the apocalypse, ol' Broussard."

"Not anymore."

"Me neither," Darby said with a sigh. "Never was much for sleepin.' Too much mischief to get into." He grinned, exposing a missing bicuspid.

"You scared?"

"Nah," Darby said, looking up from his work to gaze out into the wall of trees around them, the sky and clouds above them starting to pinken, cut by fingers of purple. "I kinda wish I could say I was, because I know that I ain't somethin' that's probably considered normal. But, I ain't ever been accused of bein' somethin' like that." Darby returned to his work.

Broussard regarded Darby, watching the man instead of what he was doing.

"Something on your mind, Crayfish?" Darby said. "I mean, aside from the obvious." He grinned again. Calm as a peeled cucumber.

Broussard didn't speak for a long time. "I just wanted to let you know that I had you all wrong."

"Do tell." Darby didn't sound the least bit surprised.

"It's just… I saw you, you know? The outside stuff. White dude. The accent. Kind of rough around the edges. All that."

"Yeah, all that."

"I had you figured for someone that you weren't."

"I get that a lot." Darby looked down his detached barrel.

"I bet you do."

"I reckon you do too," Darby said, looking through the barrel at Broussard.

"Yeah."

"Listen, man," Darby said, carefully setting aside his oil and folding his rag, then lighting up a cigarette. "I wanna say this now, cuz, well, a soul never know what tomorrow's gonna bring, you get me? So I wanna say that I think it's powerful sad the way y'all get treated, here and back in the world. I seen it. I know 'bout it. I grew up the only white kid in the colored part of town. So I get it, as much as I *can* get it."

"Yeah, I reckon you probably got it from both sides."

Darby nodded. "But be that as it may be, I can leave that part of town, put on a proper city suit and head to the other side of that dividing line that ain't marked on no map but everyone can see plain as Mary like a stripe of bright orange paint. I can walk on them streets, act like one of 'em, blend in." He spits. "I been blendin' in my entire life. Hell, I'm half a chameleon at this point. But out here, where the rules is different, governed by different judges prayin' to different gods, I can be myself, at least up to a point. We all orphans and freaks out here." Darby took several drags from his cigarette.

Broussard noticed the way Darby kept glancing over at him. He waited for him to go on, because he knew he needed to. For the first time since they'd met on the other side of the border, Darby looked nervous.

"I'm a homosexual, Broussard." Darby took a drag of his cigarette, held it in like he was hitting a joint, then exhaled.

Broussard kept his gaze on the lantern. "Yeah, you get it from all sides, all right"

Darby looked at him, then broke into a smile. "Pun intended?"

Broussard didn't get it at first, then he did. He smiled, as well. "Yeah, I guess so."

Darby laughed quietly, nodded and looked off into the jungle. "I guess so, too."

The two men sat in the loud quiet of the jungle evening, each hearing something different coming from the trees as the sun finally dipped below the horizon line, bringing its light to a different hemisphere of the earth, and leaving this one to darkness.

"Gentleman."

Darby and Broussard turned to find Chapel standing at the edge of the trees, Render, McNulty, Medrano, and Morganfield just behind him, dressed, geared, and holding their weapons.

"It's time to take our positions."

## Chapter Thirty-Five

## We the Devastating Machines

The men stand on the ridgeline above the valley, rifles ready, minds racing, hearts in throats. The mystery threatens to end them all.

I am one of the men.

I remember.

And so

here

I

am

again.

The River has brought me back here. *To here.* My past is my present and my future doesn't fucking matter now, or ever.

Present future past, past perfect nightmare.

The drain at the bottom of the world swirls with the River water of everything that has collected above it. The hound, sent here for reasons beyond my understanding, guards this drain, looking for scraps. I am one of these scraps. That is how it found me.

I am here, just as the River wants it, a passenger along for the ride of the grand nostalgia tour inside my own body, playing out the great cosmic mindfuck created to entertain whatever is watching and taking notes. I know that I will probably come back here again, and again, and again, for all eternity. This is my fate, written on this very night. It has become canon. Good God in heaven and anyone or anything else that is watching, please take me from here. I know what's coming. I can't take it again.

Chapel served me an orange. A single fucking orange, the size of a child's head.

The trees behind us—I see, I remember, I see again—stand black against the pink of the darkening sky. They're rigged with heavy speakers mounted inside black wooden boxes, spread out at intervals, bowing forward just the slightest bit with the weight of bearing these strange fruit.

Chapel stands in front of the four plus one which is me which equals five. He regards each of us with a proud, solemn look, as Morganfield walks from man to man, handing out a small plastic baggie to each one.

"What are these?" McNulty says, holding up the baggie and squinting at the two small round pieces of foam inside.

"Earplugs." Chapel says. "I'll let you know when you should use them."

The men look at each other, all formulating their own vision of what sort of horror would necessitate a total negation of sound by those issuing it.

"You don't want us to hear the tape?" McNulty says.

Chapel says nothing.

"Why can't we hear the tape?" McNulty is now asking anyone who will listen, his panic rising. "Why can't we hear it?"

The sun finally dies in the western sky. The dome above them is black at the apex and dropping slow like a curtain toward the edge of the world, peppered by the salt of a billion billion stars, most of them dead a trillion years back. Maybe I died then, too, and came back to the third planet orbiting this tiny star each and every night as the candlelight shadow of the long dead. Maybe nothing. Maybe everything.

*T. E. GRAU*

"Gentlemen, please insert your ear plugs," Chapel says.

We all do, stuffing plastic into our ears with shaky, clumsy fingers. My plugs don't fit very well, and sound leaks through the gaps. I jam my fingers into each ear in a real-time *déjà vu*, doing this again and again by habit, pushing at the plugs, hoping they'll hold this time.

"Morganfield, would you do the honors?" Chapel says. I can still see his face, as the last of the light hasn't yet be sucked from the world. He looks triumphant, and looking back with my new eyes through those old ones, Chapel looks smug, a vainglorious portrait of Varro at the dawning moments of the Battle of Cannae.

"Sir, I'd be honored," Morganfield's mouth says, the words coming seconds after the movement, the sound of his voice still making its way to my brain as it links up with an additional host. He walks to an electronic setup fixed with two reel-to-reel spools, powered by four large battery arrays stacked in the grass behind it. The back reel is full. The front is empty.

Morganfield presses a button, then steps back, cocking his .45.

Chapel puts his unlit pipe into his mouth then crosses his arms, a look of intense concentration on his face.

The fat spool spins, growing the empty one.

The shaking of my atoms and the sweat running down my head pushes one of my ear plugs free, and it falls to ground in the darkness. I don't even bother looking for it, because I know what's coming, because I remember now.

The sounds that whisper, stretch, then pour from the speakers in the trees surrounding the valley feel like tendrils of a living thing, tentacles of a huge creature buried somewhere in the ground, only showing hints of what it really is.

These are nightmares turned inside out. Roars of beasts, pushed to higher registers by male human screams that seem ripped from constricted throats seconds before death. Moans, whispers and guttural curses in two dozen Southeast Asian dialects. Chittering sounds of insects, claws and teeth scraping across polished stone. And a rumbling, throbbing bass note captured as the death rattle of a distant black star. I can't understand how anything living or mechanical could create such sounds, and don't believe anything can.

Puncturing this first wave is the high, screedling voice of Arceneaux the swamp witch, calling to me in Vietnamese from the edge of the swamp, her quivering nakedness peeking through the layer of mud, pale gray against her black skin, vines wrapped around her like a rotting shroud.

And the gnashing bark of a hound, rumbling from a massive chest. I finally hear its voice, and did before I even met it face to face. It was there the whole time, waiting for me to arrive.

The tape is transcribed as the reels spin, one diminishing as one grows, twirling twirling in the spiral that rules all things in this universe, and maybe all others.

The mad symphony of horrors continues, human utterances joined by a low register organ crash, a baritone hum lingering, as the exhortations in Vietnamese and in Lao continue, cut by screams, cackles, and howls from human and hound. Over all of this is an entreaty in a mournful child's voice, heartbreak in each word, warning all who listen. Warning them before it's too late.

This is data too big and alien to understand. The density cannot be properly absorbed and sorted. It's the soundtrack of the abyss, sung by those who swirl around its rim, mad with fear and ecstasy.

What comes out of those speakers is the most repulsive thing I've heard in my life, and yet it remains fresh and wet like an open wound, no matter how many times I'm forced to endure it.

I drop my rifle and clamp my hands over my ears. I can't hear this again. I couldn't hear it the first time, and have never been the same since.

On cue, Chapel grabs my arm and yells into my ear. "Guns up, Broussard!"

"I can't take it," I say through gritted teeth. "Not again." I don't know if this is the first time I'm saying this, or is just my line to say in this insane cosmic stage play.

"Yes, you can," Chapel says. "And you will. Take it in, and let it come right out. You have the strength."

"I can't. I can't!"

"It's not for you. It's for them," he says, pointing at the two mountains across the valley. "Don't fear that which doesn't know you."

I look at his face. I've never heard him say this before. He must have broken the chain.

He releases me and is gone. I stagger in the darkness, drowning in this horrible sound, projected out a half mile through two dozen speakers, and see activity up and down the mountains. Lights, flares, smoke of moving vehicles, the canopy of trees sway as things move past and through them.

It's working. This time it will work, and what comes next will not come. The tape continues to play, and it is working. Chapel will win his war, and everyone goes home. Everyone goes home alive.

The tape stops, and there is silence. An awful, familiar silence.

The chain has not been broken, because nothing can break the chain. What has occurred will occur, and will never stop.

"What the fuck is happening?" a voice screams. It's McNulty. "What the fuck is *happening?*"

No answer. No sound.

It's so dark I can't see my own hands. I remove my other earplug.

Then there's sound again. The sound of shells leaving long cylinders from high ground opposite our position.

"Tubes!" Render shouts from the dark.

The air fills with the whistle of plotted metal falling from the sky, then the thudding explosions as they make contact with the earth.

The darkness is gone, replaced by fire. Orange, red, yellow, white, and blue. Flares in the sky and explosions on the ground all around us. Burning phosphorus, RDX, and TNT blossom along our ridgeline like deadly tulips, cradled on cushions of smoke, showering everything with hot shrapnel and shards of earth.

The valley below is now crawling with movement as thousands leave their mountain hideaways and rush the valley floor, heading for the high ground on the other side of the bowl. Tripwires sing and claymores thud in mad syncopation. More flares cut the black sky, pink, green, and white, pushing back the stars and falling slowly like bleeding fireworks.

I find Chapel yelling something unintelligible at Morganfield in a language that may or may not be English, or even human, as Morganfield's hands dance over the audio player, making adjustments to a dead machine. I grab Chapel by the shoulders and turn him to face me.

"You need to call this in!"

"I can't," he says, the end of his words cut off by explosions. Someone screams, a sound coming from a human throat, not from a speaker.

"Why not?"

"We kill them, the mission fails."

"That doesn't make any fucking sense!"

Chapel looks out into the valley and the wave of humanity heading our way.

"Call in the strike!" I say. "You knew this would happen. You know like I do!"

Chapel's face stills, and he is about to say something, when the Hmong emerge from the trees behind us. Chapel looks at me, smiles, and pushes my rifle across my chest.

He winks. "Good luck this time."

A mortar strikes nearby, and the concussion separates us, knocking me to the ground. Shrapnel grazes my leg, my hip. I stand up and when the smoke clears, Chapel is gone.

The tape starts again, louder this time and skipping, adding an extra layer of confusion and horror to the sounds of mortars and men, rifles and bullets and screams of the dead and dying that braid together with the recorded nightmare. Now we can all hear it, but its meaning is wasted, as it's been exposed as a sham.

The first of the VC crest the ridgeline. The Hmong open up with their weapons.

I run.

## Chapter Thirty-Six

## Shedding Scales

"'*Good luck this time*,' you said. '*This time.*' Why did you say that?" I look at Chapel in the dim light of the hut, searching his face for any clue that his mouth isn't giving me. The shine in his eyes has gone flat.

"I don't remember," he says.

"That's bullshit. I remember all of it. Every second."

"Well, you would, wouldn't you?"

"What's that mean?"

"According to you, you've been there before. Experienced that night, a number of times."

"I have. You have, too. I know you have. What you said, how you said it, that look... You have, too."

"I don't think so. I don't remember...a lot of it. Most of it. I'm getting old." He looks out the small window of the hut. "The jungle takes my memories from me. A few more every day. It's why I'm here, I think. Why I stay here. I want the jungle to take all of them, and just leave me...empty."

"No, it's not that. You *do* remember. Your brain remembers, but won't let you see it. It's in there. It's all in there."

"Maybe," he says.

"Then let me fill you in."

## Chapter Thirty-Seven

## Butcherbird

I run to higher ground, away from the jungle and the ridgeline and the killing that's happening there. I need to get my feet out of the mud and post up high, wait it out and then disappear. The moon is out now, and everything is lit up blue. I can see where I'm going, and others can, too, I reckon. So I climb higher, as the eruptions of death become more faint below me.

Further up the incline, I climb the strewn boulders and granite blocks, jumping from surface to surface, surprised by my agility. Frankenstein's monster. Chapel's coward. I come to a stop on a flattop, crevices surrounding it on three sides where the stone split away when this massive stone hit the earth from wherever it was flung. Finding my feet, I turn back and look down to the fighting in the flashes of grenades and mortars. The moon is full now, the clouds have all bugged out with me, leaving the killing field illuminated and in sharp detail. I see McNulty being hacked to death with a machete. Then two, three more blades, taking off one of his arms, then his leg. Bayonets bury themselves in his torso. A barrel presses against his screaming head and takes off the top of it. He falls to the ground, dead before he lands.

Yards away Render is standing his ground in front of the wave of hateful humanity and shooting his rifle dry, then his pistol, then picks up a rock from the ground and is dropped before he can wind up.

Behind them Darby is on the move, in and out of the darkness, appearing long enough to take shots and drop weapons and pick up new ones and continue. A heavy machine gun assembled on the ridge tracks him, and begins firing as he disappears into the shadows. He doesn't emerge.

I can't find Morganfield, or Medrano. I think one of the mortar rounds got Jorge early on. It's a blur, the memory, but it's there, seen by one of my new eyes. The son of California, the father and husband and uncle and son and grandson would never mix his ingredients back into the soil of the San Joaquin.

It's Chapel I'm waiting for, because I know he's alive this time, as I'm sitting right in front of him at the other end of the River. I didn't see him before, but this time I do. He's fighting with the Hmong, his true tribe. We were hired guns, window dressing, or maybe just a part of the game I don't understand.

Dozens of VC are rushing the Hmong position, which is arrayed like a rotating shield formation, rifles firing rounds until spent, and then those behind moving to the front, while the replaced move to the back to reload and check and cool their weapons. Chapel fires his M-1 like a patient hunter taking down a herd of buffalo too far away to hear the shots.

Bodies stack up on both sides, creating a picket wall between them. The Hmong stand their ground. Chapel continues to fire. A new platoon of VC rush from the jungle to their flank, and they're caught in a half-pincer. Charlie swarms the Hmong position like ants, offering up their lives to crush the tribesmen. The last I see of Chapel he's buried by bodies, both living and dead.

My head buzzes and I swoon backward, almost losing my balance, then run into something big. I turn and find a Vietnamese man—a boy, probably, by the pudginess of his face—looking down at me, as he stands almost a foot taller. He seems surprised, not noticing me as he watched the carnage below us. His face is open, curious, full of wonder. Just like a child's. He's strapped with boxes of ammunition and bags of provisions, hundreds of pounds of it. He's a mule, not a soldier. A giant mule.

He coos and his hands reach for me. I slap them away, stepping to another boulder, stumbling over a crevasse. He takes a step forward, covering all the ground with one stride, and the hands come again, aiming for my face, the cooing getting louder, and I grab one of them, bending back the fingers. They pop, and two of them come loose from their joints.

The giant frowns and sticks out his chin shiny with drool. He forms his good hand into a fist and hits me in the ear.

The world explodes, then recedes with a keening whine, bound up with the buzzing. I grab the side of my face and red washes over my vision. I am furious. A furious one, in the flesh, and I rush at him, arms swinging wildly. My blows have no effect on the huge body, just like they don't in so many of my dreams where I have no strength, raining down punches soft as feathers on one dangerous figure after another.

He shoves me and I fall. On the ground, I kick out at his legs, and catch him on the side of the knee. The giant falls, as well, and I'm on top of him. My fists do nothing but bounce off his skin, so I claw, I bite, as we roll back and forth. When he's on top, I can't breathe, and feel the darkness closing in to take me. I scream with whatever air I have left in my lungs into his face, which gets very close to mine, his hot breath suffocating me, his teeth bared like animal. Like a dog. A giant dog perched on my chest.

A stray mortar shell whistles fast and hits nearby, and he is blown to the side, releasing me from his weight. He rolls twice and hits his head on a rock, dazing himself. I kick him in the face, breaking his nose, and he slumps onto his back. I jump on his chest and straddle his huge shape, my legs spread wide. Making a sound I never knew I had in me, and have never uttered before, I tear into his face with my fingers, digging with my nails, mashing at his damaged nose with my palm, poking out an eye with a thumb, catching the inside of his lip with three fingers and pulling with all my strength. The skin gives and rips open, a feeling that horrifies me, fuels me. His arms lift me from his chest but I redouble my efforts, grasping for his slimy tongue, reaching down into this throat, grabbing what I can of anything inside of him.

My nails push through his mouth under his tongue and I grab hold of a hard, thick bone. My other fingers join the first, and I get a firm, five-finger grip. I extend my legs and find purchase with my feet, then heave toward the sky, my hand locked inside his mouth. With a rip and then a pop, the bone comes loose, and I am flung backward with the release.

I fall on my ass, bounce, and end up on my side. The giant gets to his feet, his back to me, then slowly turns. His face is a seeping nightmare. Slime oozes from a hollow eye socket, his good eye wide, the iris black. His nose is gone, and his lips are torn back, revealing his top teeth. Below that, there is nothing but a lolling tongue, writhing like a leech through a torrent of blood, searching for something to catch it. A gurgling roar rises from his wrecked throat.

I scramble to my feet. In my hand, I hold the man's—the boy's—jawbone, teeth white through the blood, meat and connective tissue still attached.

The giant reaches out his hands, one broken, the other whole, and comes for me. I take the jawbone into my fist and meet him halfway, slashing for anything soft.

## Chapter Thirty-Eight

## South of Heaven

I look at the orange in my hand. I poke it with my thumb, but only make a dent in the skin. It doesn't tear. Chapel watches me.

"I told the people who found me, in the jungle, after, that I peeled his face like an orange."

Chapel remains silent, still processing what I just told him.

"I killed that boy, and I don't think he wanted to kill me. He was just...curious, and I killed him for it."

"We've all killed for lesser reasons."

"Yeah," I say, this stupid word not even coming close to expressing it all.

Chapel waits for me to continue.

"I killed that boy." Tears stream down my cheek as I press my thumbnail lightly into the orange, opening the skin. "I killed my brother, I think. Long time ago. I killed him, I think."

I've never told another human being not related by blood about this. Only my family knew, and that was narrowed to a select few. My daddy knew, which is why he left. Never laid a hand on me for it. He never had to, because the removal of his eyes from me that day forward hurt more than any hands he could have put on me. After my daddy left, my momma left, too, in a different way. Just faded and faded until she wasn't there anymore. Then it was just me and my grandmother, but she didn't know. Or if she did, she never told me, or acted like it, all the way until she was taken from me, too, tongue sticking out like a strangled bird.

"I killed my brother, I think. Long time ago. Then I killed that boy on the rocks. Stuffed his body into a hole and left him there, and then I ran until everything went black."

The tears stream hot, expelling years of guilt and shame and rage. They burn my cheeks.

"Those eyes found me when I woke up. At the edge of the jungle, way back in the fog. Yellow. Looking at me. *Knowing* me, what I'd done. So I ran again."

The jawbone is now in my other hand. Chapel looks at it, then back at me. "I've been carrying this around for five years," I say. "This and all of it. And I ain't had a good day or night's rest ever since that time on the rocks."

"I'm sorry," Chapel says. "About all of it."

"Fuck you."

That's fair," he says. "You're angry.""

"Angry? Nah, I'm fucking *furious.*" The gun itches in my waistband. I've never wanted to kill a man more in my life.

"I suppose you are."

"Why did you lead us out there? There were hundreds of them. *Thousands.* We were sitting ducks. Everyone died. Medrano, Render, McNulty, Darby..."

"Not everyone."

"Everyone," I insist. "Except maybe you."

He looks away, brows furrowed, holding something inside his eyes.

"What happened?" I say, almost pleading.

"Tactical error."

"How did you think that would ever work?"

"I believed in a belief," Chapel says, turning back to me, more sure with his words now that he's back on message. That old bullshit message.

"I had faith in faith."

He's trying to be clever, and I almost gag. "Faith dies when it meets a bullet," I say. "Lead and iron cure faith real fucking fast."

"No they don't. Lead and iron make it stronger."

"It didn't out there, on that night."

"Something went wrong…" he says, a twitch shooting up the side of his face. He rubs it.

"*You* went wrong, and we all paid for it."

"You don't think I've paid?" he says, rising to his feet, his voice elevating with him. "You don't think I've suffered each and every second of my life since then? The dead have it easy. They just disappear into nothing. It's the living that go on suffering."

"They don't disappear," I say, thinking back to the French house, to every waking moment since I came to after they found me in wandering, half mad, in a Thai jungle. "Not all of them." I slump back, dropping the orange. It rolls on the clay floor and disappears into the shadows of a corner.

Chapel begins pacing, his words taking on a rehearsed speed, called forward from many years ago. He's not listening to me, lost in his old playbook. "We'd used it before, Operation Wandering Soul, and it'd worked in limited applications. We'd play on the Vietnamese belief of the Wandering Soul, where if a soldier was killed far from his homeland, and his remains weren't returned and buried on his family's land, his soul, his ghost, would wander forever."

Thoughts of the old woman, the girl. "They all believe that?"

"Most of them. It's an old Buddhist thing. Every year, they celebrate Vu Lan Day, an absolution for the soul, allowing all the wandering souls to come home if the remains are recovered and returned. They make shrines, set them free on the water."

"The river on fire…"

Chapel nods. "We recorded a tape in Hanoi, calling in engineers from all over, sound effects experts, theater people, actors and actresses. Some old Hollywood buddies. Big production. Lots of eggheads and spiritualists brought in as consultants. Once the script was written, we put it on tape, with the voices of ghosts warning the VC that if they died away from home, in Laos, let's say, their souls would wander, and they'd never find peace in the afterlife. The tape was good. One of the finest creations of the Central Intelligence Agency. It worked in small numbers, controlled tests on apartment blocks, villages, then we went wide with it at Nui Ba Den Mountain in '70. Rooted out a hundred and fifty die-hard NVA without firing a shot. That's what gave me the idea. When something works small, you build it out and it can work big. Scaling-up. It's the nature of chemistry, business, cooking, whatever. A precisely controlled increase dedicated to a fixed ratio. You drop poison gas on three people, they die. You drop poison gas on a thousand people, they die just like the three."

"It wasn't poison gas we were letting loose out there."

"It was worse. It was nightmares. A destruction of heaven."

"Charlie didn't seem to agree."

He shrugged. "Like I said, tactical error."

"More like a technical one."

He doesn't say anything.

"Why did the tape stop?" I ask the question that's festered inside me for half a decade.

"Pardon?"

"The tape. It stopped. Why did it stop?"

He looks at me with those gray eyes. In the low light of the hut, I think I see him smile. "Technical error," he repeats.

I get to my feet. "So that's it, huh? That's the story? Stupid plans goes to shit and all your men slaughtered, with the ending being you living up here like some great white god? Charming the native with baubles and trinkets? Sky magic and nightmares on tape?"

"Don't give me that bullshit. You know me better than that."

"No, actually I don't. I don't know you at all. I thought I might have, but realized I don't know a fucking thing about you. If I did..."

"What? You would have stayed in that cell? Been shipped back stateside for a nice court martial for cowardice in the field and dragged ass to your hometown in shame?"

"So you did me a favor?"

"I allowed you to do yourself a favor."

"Did you do a favor to Render? To Medrano? To Darby?"

"And to McNulty and Morganfield, too. I allowed all of you to fight for something right, for something that had value, meaning."

"And to die like sheep. Scared and confused and overrun by wolves come down from the mountain."

"To die with honor."

"There's no honor in dying. Just death."

"But not in your case," Chapel says, eyes narrowing. "You're afraid to die."

"I am. But not for the reason you think."

"No, I think it *is* for the reason I think."

"You don't know shit," I say, the tears welling again. This time born from the frustration of unending fear that no one can see.

"You're shaking," he says, in that tone I remember. "You've been shaking since you got here."

I don't say anything. I can't help it. My limbs need chemicals, and they're not getting the proper amount. They're rebelling.

He looks into my face. "But you're not afraid."

"Not of you."

"What happened to you?" he says, voice hushed with some weird sense of curiosity and wonder. Still the boy who needs to know. To see. "Afterwards, I mean."

"I brought a dog back from the jungle," I say, holding up my other hand, clutching what was in my other pocket. "And this is its bone."

Chapel isn't sure what I mean, but leans forward to learn.

"I need to bury it for him."

T . E .   G R A U

## Chapter Thirty-Nine

## Moons at Your Door

Chapel and I stand in the village clearing, each of us with a pack of gear at our feet. I wonder if this place has a name, or appears on any map, but knowing Chapel, I realize the question is ridiculous.

Aside from Sua, who speaks a few low, terse words to Chapel and then walks away without a look in my direction, no one comes out to see us off. Not a sound comes from any of the huts.

I look down to the far end of the village. All the windows and doorways and porches are empty. Not a human or dog in sight. It's a ghost town.

"Where's your wife?" I say.

He sighs. "She won't come out."

"Why?"

"Because she doesn't believe that I'm coming back. If she doesn't say goodbye, I'll never have left."

I think about this for a few moments. "Is that what marriage is like?"

"It is for me," he says with a grin. The radio in his hand crackles. He speaks into it, muttering a few words in Hmong.

"What was that?" I say.

"Our rides are coming."

"Chopper?"

"Not quite."

"Jeep?"

He smiles at me again. "Tanks."

## Chapter Forty

## The Fire in our Throats Will Beckon the Thaw

We ride on the backs of mountains, each of us, moving as the mountain moves. I am astride an elephant, and it feels like a dream. This was the mode of eastern kings, and for a brief second, I close my eyes, fill my lungs, and feel like one.

When I allow my eyes to open, we are far into the wilderness again. An ocean of trees and clouded blue skies broken occasionally by farms and patches of ruined ground, dead trees that stand out like burnt bones arranged against a blanket of green that slowly tries to cover it out of slow-motion sadness. It's impossible to forget the war here, in a country where it wasn't officially fought, no matter how hard all of us involved might try.

To my left I see the partially buried wreckage of a burned-out American bomber jutting up at the edge of an abandoned rice paddy not yet reclaimed by the land. The jungle licked at the crumpled outer hull, tasting it and deciding to come back to it later. Long swaths of moss cover the jagged parts that stick out into the air, giving shaggy beards to twisted metal.

"One of ours?" I say.

Chapel nods. "Douglas B-66. One of our Easter bunnies, sent to drop all the eggs."

"Eggs?"

He gestures to a tiny farming village adjacent to the field, just up from the path. Children play, while others stand in a line, watching us with fascination. Some smile and call out, holding up two fingers. Others, the ones leaning on crude crutches or absently itching at a stump that stops at their elbow, shoot us hard looks. It's impossible to forget the war here.

"What happened to them?" I say.

"Cluster bombs. The country is covered with them, buried in the ground, waiting to go off, like hidden Easter eggs."

Our two mountains carry us past the children. Those that can run give chase. The others turn their backs.

"Every day, someone steps on one, or digs it from the ground and plays catch, maybe a little soccer. Then..." Chapel gestures toward them. "That's our legacy in Laos, Broussard. That and a hundred thousand wandering souls."

"Were you involved in that? The bombing missions?"

"We all were. The buck never stops in a secret war."

I look down at the kids smiling up at us, saying something in Lao. Laughing and pointing. I don't understand it, but I'm pretty sure Chapel does. "Is that why you never left? Because you felt like you owed them something?"

"Is that why you didn't leave?"

"I did leave. I laid low in Bangkok."

"No, you didn't. You're still here, with the rest of us," Chapel says, looking at the children, who slow down, stop, and head back to their village. "Waiting."

## Chapter Forty-One

## Everything You Need

We've ridden for most of the day, but the sun doesn't seem to move in the sky. Maybe we're moving with it, in some perfect imitation dance to keep the nighttime at bay. Chapel and I haven't said a word to each other since we saw the children. I keep looking behind us, up off the trail into the jungle and the stands of trees when there's a break in the wilderness, wondering what's following us, moving from shadow to shadow. Knowing that I'm being followed, but not sure by what anymore. It feels like many things, a legion on my trail.

Chapel abruptly stops his elephant, or what counts for abrupt from a six-ton animal. I slow mine to a halt, as well, with much less success. I never was good at riding.

"What is it?" I say, my mount stomping and fussing. It doesn't like me. Animals never did.

"Look," he says, and gestures upward with his chin.

I follow his direction and see the twin mountain peaks girded in vegetation, the V carved between, making them. Down below is the river that burned that night, lighting up the way for us to unleash Chapel's doomed experiment to win the war.

"This is it," I say, my voice stilled by certainty as much as wonder.

"Yes, it is."

I look around in every direction, trying to familiarize myself based on spotty memories. I hear the river now, and am not sure if it's coming from inside me, or down in the valley. This worries me, because one of them might take me away from the other just as I've finally arrived.

"Can you find it?"

I look at Chapel.

"The place," he says.

"I think so."

Chapel points. "We were set up all along that ridgeline, so use that as a guide. A starting point."

I get down off my elephant, it waiting patiently as I do so without much grace. Chapel tosses me a wad of fabric. I shake it out. It's a woven grass bag, large and sturdy.

"What's this for?"

"To carry what you find."

The reality of the situation begins to creep up on me, and the realization that what I'm looking for might not be here, or I might not be able to find it. Both options are too harrowing to contemplate, so I shake them off and busy myself with inspecting my gear and provisions, meager as they are. Nothing in my pack will take me very far, including the pistol.

"You have everything you need?" Chapel asks.

I hold up the jawbone. Chapel regards it grimly. He is the only one outside of the cave, outside of me, who has ever seen it. It hasn't been in the sun for a long, long time.

He nods once. "Good enough."

I turn to the high ground, then to Chapel. "If I'm not back... If I don't *come* back..."

Chapel waits for me to finish. I don't, changing the angle instead. "If I don't say goodbye, I've never left."

"Then let's not," he says. "We need you in this world."

He says no more. I can tell he's done talking. Maybe he's been done for years, which is why he came out here, to Laos, to live out the remainder of his clock and to die in silence, without having to talk about it to those who would demand that he tell his story. I'm done talking, too. I've said my piece.

"Thanks, sir," I say.

"It's the least I can do, Specialist Broussard."

I look down at the jawbone, turn it over in my hand. I remember looking at it in the jungle, when I was on the move, heading toward nowhere that brought me to Thailand, then to Bangkok, and then right back here. I'm remembering more things now, away from the cave and the things done there, which scares me, *thrills* me. I'm starting to remember how it was before, and it makes the now all the more wretched. So much wasted everything.

The teeth are white and straight. There are burn marks on the bone from where I charred off the muscle and sinew. The meat. I couldn't leave it behind, bury it in the mud. I had to have a trophy, a memento that told me that I finally became a killer. A real man. A good soldier. The shame of that has murdered me a little more each night since then.

I grip the sharp bone tightly in my hand, and give one last look to Chapel, who clamps his grandfather's pipe between his teeth.

Then I set off up the hill, gaining ground, elevation.

## Chapter Forty-Two

## The 21st Chapter

I move from boulder to boulder to slab, my legs feeling stronger, feet searching for the right spot, while I survey the ridgeline below where my unit all died that night. Well, not all of it, as Chapel said. It looks different during the day, and five years on. The natural world has reclaimed the blood and bodies, erased the holes in the ground dug by exploding shells and filled them with living green. It seems a strange violation of the recovered peace to remember the horror of what happened here that night, so I ask the jungle forgiveness for my trespasses.

I keep moving, climbing higher, until my feet stop me. They've found it before my eyes have a chance. In front of me is a gap in the arrangement of rock, just large enough for a man—or the body of a smiling mule—to fit. I'd know this place in my sleep, as one does the familiar terrain of a recurring dream, which are the only dreams I've known since my rebirth on these rocks.

I peer down into the space between the two boulders, and see only moss and a wet blackness below. I get down on my hands and knees, like a Malay Muslim in prayer, and press my face to the opening. My eyes see nothing. My old eyes. My new eyes see it. See them. A collection of bones, withered by time, twisted by weather, and picked clean by the insects of the jungle. Jumbled yellow parts of a complicated puppet. They're big bones. Those of a giant.

I reach my arm in to grab the nearest bone, but my fingers don't reach. I'm going to have to go down there.

I was ready to be terrified, slithering into that tight space, clawing my way into my bloody, freak-out past. But I'm not afraid, I realize, almost as an afterthought, too busy figuring out the logistics of fitting myself in. I make myself into the snake, and get to slithering.

The opening is tight, but I squeeze through, scratching both sides of my body, which isn't much more than a stuffed scarecrow these days, ratty with old skin. Freeing my legs and feet, I drop down into a small, hollowed-out compartment, and drag my pack behind me. This is my first time here, as I never entered that night, just shoved what I had done down a hole, as if that would erase the act and exonerate me for eternity. Out of sight and off the books. Fat fucking chance. The past has a way of showing up like a bad penny, jangling at the bottom of your pocket until you're driven out of your mind, or at least as far as Bangkok.

The bones rest on a shelf higher up from the floor, near the fissure, waiting for me at eye level as I crouch. I can touch them now, and do, expecting something akin to a bee sting. But they're just bones, damp and cold from the dark. I move my hands through them, finding something round at the back of the pile.

He rotted away facing the wall, like a punished schoolboy.

I remove the skull that falls free from the spine with a dry clatter, and turn it to face me. All of the teeth of the maxilla are intact, wide and gleaming white. The bottom part is missing.

With my free hand I reach into my pack and pull out my shameful memento from that savage night. I hold up the jawbone and fasten it under the temporal plate, completing the skull. A full set of teeth smile at me, black-hole eyes not giving away if the grin is one of madness or mirth, or murder. None of this feels like Shakespeare, and none of the world is a stage, because the actors don't die in a play.

"I'm sorry," I say. "For all of it."

The skull says nothing, and I'm glad it doesn't.

I emerge from the tiny catacomb, bring up my pack and the bag full of bones. The sun is beating down brightly now, the early clouds chased off to the horizon. I squint up into the sky, then look down at the boonie hat in my hand. It's empty, all of its teeth gone. I tent it open with my fist, then put it on my head, the brim shading my eyes. It barely fits over my hair, but it fits.

I look down the hillside toward the path, where I'd left Chapel and the elephants, but all of them are gone. I knew this would be the case, even though I was hoping I'd be wrong. I wanted to talk to him a little more, if he was willing, about this and a lot of things. All those things I wish I'd asked and said, but he's just a ghost now like the rest of them, and was heading back home.

I work my way down from atop the boulders and stand on the hillside, overlooking the valley and the river that once burned, ringed by the ridgeline that burned even hotter, soaked with the blood of that terrible night of horrors. The river would be set ablaze again soon, when the season was right, from now until the very end of things. Each flame a tribute to a wandering soul that wasn't forgotten by those left behind. Hopefully there would be less this year, and less the year after. With any luck, there'd be one less flame on some other river further to the east very soon. Or as soon as I could find a place to properly bury what was I was carrying.

The bones in the bag rattle as they shift. I hold them up, hoping they'll tell me something. A direction. An acceptance of my apology. But they don't. Bones don't speak. They're only spoken for.

I lower the bag and look across the valley, toward the twin mountains. On the far end, just outside the tree line, Black Shuck rests on its haunches, watching me.

We regard each other, the valley stretching out between us, the river flowing silently down below.

Black Shuck stands, turns and begins to walk, its corded muscles gently rolling with powerful ease, shining in the sunlight. It stops after a few yards and turns its massive head back to me, tongue lolling over its long teeth, just like a dog. Not a hound. But a dog.

I shoulder my pack and collect my bag, contents clinking together with a peculiar music like marimba keys, and walk around the rim of the valley, heading toward the dog.

Black Shuck turns and walks again, slowly enough for two human legs to keep up. It's heading east, the sun tells me. *It's heading to Vietnam*—the bones tell me, mute no more—to where it was born, to where he was born, and where both of them need to return, to rest, and to die.

The dog is heading in the direction of the River, and so am I, traveling to where the water drains into the Great Nothing that waits for everything that escaped but eventually finds its way home.

Our steps find the rhythm of the other, four legs and two and two more in the bag, and we walk together, not side by side, but moving in the same direction, just like always. But this time, neither of us runs. We let the current take us.

## About the Author

T.E. Grau is the author of the books *They Don't Come Home Anymore*, *Triptych: Three Cosmic Tales*, *The Lost Aklo Stories*, *The Mission*, and *The Nameless Dark* (nominated for a 2015 Shirley Jackson Award for Single-Author Collection), whose work has been published in various platforms around the world, translated into Spanish, Italian, German, and Japanese. Grau lives in Los Angeles with his wife and daughter, and is currently working on his second collection and second novel.

CPSIA information can be obtained
at www.ICGtesting.com
Printed in the USA
LVHW041729080119
603164LV00007B/1019/P